Stormy seas, a captive heart, and a coupling that breaks all the rules...

After years of committed service, Captain William "Bump" Quinn has finally taken the helm of the pirate ship Scarlet Night. But when rough waters send the Night off course, William winds up shipwrecked and alone on enemy shores—and prisoner to China's most powerful pirate queen.

Captain Jian Jun is as alluring as she is formidable, and she's careful not to let anyone too close. But the silence of the handsome Jamaican pirate in her custody intrigues her. Tempted by his topaz eyes and the strength of his character, she allows the captive into her inner sanctum. Though their bond defies all convention, Jun finds she is powerless against the emotions Will stirs in her. She prays their first union will not be her last. But with danger lurking in unexpected places, her beloved pirate may soon get the chance to prove he is every inch the hero he seems in her arms . . .

Visit us at www.kensingtonbooks.com

Books by Lisa Olech

Captains of the Scarlet Night
Within A Captain's Hold
Within A Captain's Treasure
Within A Captain's Fate
Within A Captain's Power
Within A Captain's Soul

Published by Kensington Publishing Corporation

Within A Captain's Soul

A Captains of the Scarlet Night Novel

Lisa Olech

LYRICAL PRESS
Kensington Publishing Corp.
www.kensingtonbooks.com

To Jenny

Author's Foreword

I never set out to write Bump's story, but he not only grew up on the deck of the Scarlet Night, he grew in my heart and the hearts of those who came to "know" him. Writing a hero like him stretched me as a writer and opened my mind and heart to a new community of caring, generous people. I hope I have honored their trust in me to make Captain William "Bump" Quinn a hero that many will love and few will forget.

Acknowledgments

As always, thanks go to Kensington, Lyrical and their amazing team for their continued faith in my stories. To the best editor on the planet, Amanda.

Thank you, Dawn, for your support and wisdom.

I need to thank Kathy Hills, Christyne Butler, and the Plot Bunnies for saving Bump from the perils of living at the whim and fate of my pen!

Thanks to Gwen, Michelle, Lauren, Patrick and all those with a personal investment in this book.

Thanks to my readers who have made this series so successful.

And to my family who is growing more wonderful with each passing year.

I love you all!

Chapter 1

William Quinn hated the dark. His companion had taken the lantern when she left. He could still smell the spiced honey of her skin and the musk of their sex in the rumpled sheets. She'd been a tiger in bed. His flesh still burned where her nails had raked his back. He'd lost himself for an hour or two between her smooth dark thighs. He only wished he'd learned her name.

Will lay in the bed and closed his eyes to the darkness. It was easier to visualize the layout of the room from memory this way. The door was to starboard. A three-drawer chest sat a foot to port. His pants were another matter. Where had she tossed them? She'd been in a terrible hurry to put her mouth on him. When she'd stripped him and seen his engorged cock, a smile spread across her shining face as if she'd discovered some long lost treasure. After that, she was driven by a single-minded desire. She'd been a most eager partner.

He rose and found his pants along with the wide blood-red sash he wore about his waist. And one boot. All the while, his limited sense was still on high alert. In this darkness, it would be easy to hide and ambush him. It wasn't as if he'd hear anyone approaching, but having lost his hearing at such a young age, over his lifetime, he'd honed his other senses to razor sharp. Will lifted his nose and gave another sniff. No, he was alone.

The heat along this stretch of the world limited his choice of clothing. Bare chested, he slipped into a tooled leather vest. He patted the breast pocket. His lusty partner wasn't interested in his winnings from tonight's poker tables. As the daughter of one of the local pepper merchants, money was not what she longed for. Madagascar pepper was considered black gold along this great treasure route. Her father was one of the wealthiest men in the city.

Will found his other boot, and sat on the edge of the bed to slip them on his feet. He sat there for a long moment. The hollow beating of his heart echoed in his chest. Even after hours of pleasure, the only thing sated was his body.

This girl, whoever she was, hadn't been interested in his newfound wealth or even knowing who he was. She'd only been interested in lying with him. It was the same wherever he went these days. He'd become a novelty.

Sex with the silent man.

It wasn't as if he could brag about his conquests. Tell tales of your night in his bed. He wouldn't bore you with long stories, or shout demands. He was deaf and never learned the basic fundamentals of speech. For some reason that made women eager to spread their legs for him. At least for one meaningless night.

Making his way to the door, Will wasn't surprised to find the public rooms below still doing a brisk business. Time held no meaning to these establishments. Glancing toward the back corner, the poker game still wore on. He was tempted to add to his already bulging purse. Tonight's profits had come too easy, but then it had always been a talent of his to read faces. Call it a lucrative byproduct of being deaf. Whether bluffing at cards or dealing with his crew, he could spot a liar at fifty yards.

Will's long legs carried him quickly through the dangerous dark streets. At more than six and a half feet tall, he made an imposing figure. The three-pistol baldric and side cutlass helped. As did his permanent scowl. He pulled a short knife from a leather sheath and carried it at his side. For two reasons. A handy weapon was never a bad idea, and the high polish on the blade gave him the perfect view of anyone trying to approach him from behind.

Will reached the docks without incident and was finally able to breathe easy when he dropped down upon the polished decks of the *Scarlet Night*. The gentle tip of the boards shifting beneath his feet, the smell of tarred rigging, and the sight of her three thick masts brought a smile to his face. He was home.

'Captain.' His first mate, Griffin, tapped his shoulder to sign the word before giving Will a sharp salute. Will returned the salute and replied with a few quick hand signals of his own.

'Are we ready to leave at first light?'

Griffin nodded. Will scanned the deck in a slow sweep. All looked as it should. The crew was busy loading supplies of food and ale. Barrels of powder and crates of spices were all being stowed properly.

Will slapped Griffin's shoulder in praise. He was a good man. Smart. Responsible. And a damn fine pirate. He could filet a ship with a single cannon shot down the length of their hull and fight like a man possessed. Short yet sturdy, his strength coiled in him like a taught spring waiting to unleash its controlled power. Will was happy he was on their side.

'Problems?'

His first mate shook his head. Thankfully, Griffin was quick to pick up the basic hand signals Will had adapted over the years to help him communicate. Between the use of bells and signs and gestures, Will had been able to build a crew that could follow his strict orders and knew exactly what was asked of them and when. No small feat, but after almost two years at the helm, he'd amassed a fine group of men...and one woman.

He recalled the day he'd become Captain of the *Scarlet Night*. He and the former captain, Tupper Quinn, had literally stolen their ship back from under the nose of the British Navy. They'd been captured and faced hanging for crimes against the crown, but what the wool-backed Brits hadn't counted on was the fact that not only did Tupper have friends in high places with deep pockets, but Will had a hide thicker than a bull elephant. He still had the scars to prove it.

Three months after their escape, as they made their way down the west coast of Africa, skirting the British at every turn, hiding in every nook and cranny along the rugged coastline, Tupper broke the news that she no longer wished to be called Captain.

'It's yer turn now. Ye've earned it. The Scarlet Night *is in yer blood. She's yer soul. Hell, ye cut yer teeth on the riggin.' It's only right to pass her on to you now.'*

At first, he'd laughed at her. She was talking crazy. Who ever heard of a deaf captain? But as time went on Tupper cleverly stepped back little by little. With each new crewmember they acquired, she planted the seeds of possibility. By giving him more responsibility, more of her power, she opened the path for him to finally take command.

It was only then he learned the real reason why Tupper Quinn was stepping aside.

The muscle in his jaw tensed at the thought. He turned back to Griffin. *'How is she?'*

Griffin jerked his chin toward the ladder way. *'In her cabin.'*

Will made his way below deck to the rear of the ship. He'd swiped two bottles of her favorite rum from the galley as he passed. He knocked on the thick wood of her door, but didn't wait to feel her stomp on the floorboards to indicate he could enter.

The Captain's quarters. Oak trimmed and impressive. Built-in cupboards and a carved niche holding the bed. The choicest plunder filled chests and trunks flanking the walls. A wide swath of diamond-paned windows followed the back curve of the ship's fantail. The polished floors now boasted a bright rug secured from a Persian ship.

While Will came here daily to work the logs and charts, it was still and always would be Tupper's quarters. He found her in bed, half sitting, half reclining. She was the color of a dirty sail. When he placed the bottles on the desk, she opened her eyes.

She straightened and ran a hand over her dull hair. *'Bump, there you are. Where did you run off to?'*

The old nickname made him smile. She was the only one to call him that anymore, and continued to do so when they were alone. He'd been given the name when he'd first come aboard. A filthy, spindly urchin rescued from the fetid gutters of Port Royal, Jamaica. Imagine a deaf child on a pirate ship. How he survived was a true miracle.

In the beginning, he was always in the wrong place at the wrong time with ropes flying and blocks swinging. Needless to say, he couldn't hear anyone warning him to look out or duck. It had taken weeks before he developed a sixth sense that something was about to cleave his skull in two. Until then, he had more knots and scrapes. His face spent more time on the deck boards than his feet. Earned the name Bump. As with fool nicknames, it bloody well stuck and followed him clear into adulthood.

But when Tupper made the decision to give up her commission, they agreed Captain Bump was not a fit name anymore. As it was, when Gavin Quinn, Tupper's late husband and former Captain of the *Scarlet Night,* brought Bump aboard, none knew his surname. An old woman claiming to be the boy's grandmother had pleaded with Gavin to save him from the brutal life he was living on the street of Port Royal. She'd told Gavin his given name was William.

Against all advice, Gavin Quinn had taken him on as a fledgling cabin boy who could neither speak nor understand and who spent more time those first few days bleeding from the head than performing any duties. But Gavin became like a father to him and saved his life. Will would forever regret not being able to save his. Captain Gavin Quinn died in the great earthquake of 1692 that wiped most of Port Royal, Jamaica off the map. Will witnessed the whole horrific event. Watched the sea swallow the land. Helpless and heartbroken. He still remembered every detail of that awful day as if it happened yesterday.

Will's surname Quinn was a gift from Tupper. He and the rest of the crew were arrested for treason and piracy by the British. Not right to hang a man with half a name. All those years he'd been like a son to Gavin and Tupper. When it came time to sign his death warrant, Tupper made it official. He was a Quinn—at least 'til they set him swinging.

'Pour me some rum, and tell me where you've been.' Tupper gestured as she swept her thin, pale legs over to hang off the side of her bed. She was looking frailer by the day. She pulled the shoulder of her shirt from drooping down her arm. Will handed her a mug. She downed the strong drink in one swallow and held her mug out for more. He refilled it. Gladly. They repeated this once more. It was taking more rum these days to ease her pain. He'd feed her a barrel full if it meant she'd rest comfortably.

Tupper patted his hand and leaned back against the pillows. Will stowed the bottle as he eyed the charts spread out over the desk. There was no question in his mind. His original plan was not going to work.

With the route he'd drawn out, they'd never reach China in time. He would have to risk crossing paths with the British and navigate the Indian Ocean then through the treacherous Malacca Straights past Singapore. These were unfamiliar waters, but what choice did he have?

Tupper started to cough. Her body wracked with each bark. She covered her mouth with a handkerchief to whip the bloody spittle from her mouth. Seeing the blood, Will's stomach dropped. His hands curled into fists.

He had learned about the progressive medicines now available in China. They were far ahead of western doctors. He'd get her there no matter the cost. Will prayed their luck would hold. They'd survived the harrowing trip around the Cape of Good Hope, hadn't they? It had been the quickest way coming west, and Will had accidently discovered a small unknown secret to navigating the *'Cape of good storms'* without losing a single life.

Tupper rapped her mug on the edge of the desk asking for more rum. Will pulled the bottle and then poured her some more. They'd fought the beast of Good Hope, and it was that hope he was hanging on to now. There was one life he was determined not to lose. Not if he had any say in the matter.

Will raised the wick on the lantern and studied the maps. Time was the enemy now. If he didn't find the fastest route to China, Tupper would soon be dead.

Chapter 2

A red sun rose out of a fiery sea. It was the time of reckoning. Jian Jun sat in her place of honor upon a gold-trimmed throne. Around the perimeter of the room stood her seconds-in-command, advisors, scribes, keepers of her vast accounts. With a fleet numbering in the hundreds of ships, it took an entire nation to oversee the operation. Jian Jun was their captain and supreme authority. She was their pirate queen.

As queen, each appointed commander came before her to pay homage and deliver to her the hearty percentage due from his or her rich bounty. Disputes came before her to be settled. Punishments, swift and severe were delivered as well. Although not delivered by her own hand, her wrath was ruthless according to many. She demanded a strict adherence to her rules, and was intolerant of those who broke them. You didn't build an empire this size by being weak.

General Chou Peng—her right hand, first mate, her iron fist—stood nearby. He wore the purple of royalty. A symbol that he was honored as her confidant and trusted as her second in command. Peng was a study of angles. Sharp shoulders, chiseled cheek bones, pointed face made more severe by the thin blade of black beard decorating his chin. He was sleek, refined, cold. Not a tall man, yet he carried himself with an air of utter control and authority.

Peng's loyalty was absolute. Rather remarkable considering she had been the one who'd taken over her husband's fleet known to all as the Dragon's Fire. Many were more than shocked on the day she appeared before them wearing her late husband's ill-fitting armor and literally stepped into his boots. Peng had been the obvious successor, but Jian Jun was determined to use the knowledge she had gleaned at Jian Fu's powerful elbow. She would not return to the life he had rescued her from, and would fight whomever she must to honor his memory and rule his pirate empire.

One of her sub captains, the commander of the junk, *Yue 'er Gao*, was dragged before her in shackles and forced to kneel at her feet. Twenty of his men were hauled into a huddled mass behind him, their ankles chained one to another.

Chou Peng read the petition levied against the captain and his crew. They were charged with disobeying Jian Jun's direct order and attacking a small fishing village under her protection. As if those offenses alone were not cause to lose their heads, they had assaulted the innocents—women, children, elders. Burned their homes. Ransacked their farms. Butchered their livestock.

The commander stood and held her stare. He had stood with the same indignant air once before and showed the evidence of her justice. The last time he had lost only his left ear as punishment for not listening to the laws. Today he would lose much more.

"He openly defies me." Jun spoke to Chou Peng in English as to keep their conversation private. "Disrespects me. Leads his men completely outside our rules with no shame and no conscience."

"Headstrong, yes, but his ship is one of the most profitable."

Her voice rose, and yet she never broke her dark stare upon the prisoner. "He attacked people I gave my word to protect. Do you believe I place gold above human life? The life of a child? The honor of a woman?"

"Of course not," Peng placated. "The report of the incident speaks of vast amounts of alcohol involved. Perhaps they were not in their right minds."

"I should excuse the raping and total destruction of this humble peaceful village to a night of drunken madness?" Jun held up a gloved hand to cease any further discussion. "No." She rose to her feet, pulling both scimitars that hung in crossed leather baldrics across her chest. Raising the blade of one she slashed it through the air and pointed its barbed end at the man's throat.

In her native Chinese, she pronounced sentence, never easing her stony glare. "I want his ear, his tongue, his hands, then his head. And the heads of all the cowards who followed him like blind sheep to commit this atrocity against me, this fleet, and my people." Her voice thundered through the room. "Let them be a warning to all, that my word is law and my justice fierce. Decorate the rails of the *Yue 'er Gao* with the bloody remains. Adorn the harbor with their heads before burning the junk into the sea."

Chou Peng stepped forward and ordered the guards to remove the men to be executed. He gave Jun a short sharp bow before he followed the convicted men out to see to the deed set before him. Jun, watching them go, never broke, never moved. The arm holding the sword remained steady. Yet inside she trembled with a mixture of outrage and fear and numbing sadness.

It wasn't until she returned to the sanctuary of her private quarters that she crumbled. Jun banished her maid before pulling off the elaborate headdress and tossing it aside. She tore at the black chest plate of armor covering her front, constricting her breath, crushing her heart.

Visions of the village the men attacked ran through her mind. The handsome homes, and farms, the gentle, hardworking people. Their beautiful faces. She sank onto the floor, covering her own face with her hands. The scenes in her mind quickly morphed into those of her own village. It, too, had been attacked by vicious pirates. She had watched as her parents had been killed. She, her sister, and every other young woman were then dragged away and sold into lives of prostitution and slavery.

Jun had been one of the fortunate ones who escaped being raped that horrific day. And who, because of her comely face, had been spared. As a virgin, her purity was seen as a choice commodity.

She never saw her sister again. Where she was or if she was even alive, she didn't know. Jun's body and virtue sold for a high price to an infamous brothel in Singapore. The Palace of Painted Pleasures. There, rebellious whores tattooed themselves in bold, colorful art as a defiant act against the carnal dishonoring of their bodies. It became their source of pride instead. Their inked flesh becoming more ornate with each passing year, as almost a measure of their experience and age. They became renowned for it, and desired by scores of men seeking to rut between their decorated thighs.

Jun was initiated into this brothel and prepared for the day she, too, would be forced to sell her body. She remembered weeping for all she had lost, and the humiliating prospect of such a disreputable life. Ornamental women, their skin covered in bold and striking colors, stripped her, bathed her, and shaved her before holding her down as she fought against the pain of a thousand needles. They decorated her hairless mound with a beautiful blooming lotus flower. Her first tattoo in stunning pinks, blues, and brown. The lotus was to symbolize the purity and ownership of her body. For out of the mud and muck, the lotus rises and blooms clean of any filth. They told her it also stood as a symbol of detachment. For as in nature droplets of water easily slide off the lotus blossom's petals. It was her reminder to rise above what was being done to her body, and to remain pure in her mind. Jun would carry the private agony and beauty of that ink at the apex of her thighs forever.

It took several weeks for her flesh to heal and for her to complete her instruction in the fine art of sexual pleasures. She learned how to use her mouth and her sex to bring clients to climax quickly. The words of encouragement and seduction used to tantalize each partner. Her skin buffed, smoothed, and creamed. Her hair oiled to shine like the long feathered wing of a raven. They painted her face, and taught Jun how to make sure no child would ever grow in her womb.

Soon, it was time. Draped in lengths of transparent silks, Jun paraded before a choice group of men, all willing to pay the highest price to lay claim to her virginity. Dignitaries, princes, sultans, powerful rich men began bidding for her. It took every bit of courage not to disgrace herself and vomit on her feet.

Then she saw him. Jian Fu.

He was different from the rest. Reserved in his austere leather clothing, he stood to the side in silence as the frenzy of bidding continued. When the last bid had been made, Jian Fu stepped forward and offered three times the amount. He hadn't waited for the commotion to settle down before he threw a stack of money upon the auction table and forcibly dragged her from the room.

He'd covered her with a blanket and, in silence, led her out of the brothel.

Frightened and in shock she tugged at him to release her. "Where are you taking me?"

"Anywhere but here," he snapped.

Where he took her still surprised her to this day. Painted and tattooed as a common whore, wearing little but scarves, wrapped in a garish quilt of pieced satins, she stood next to him as a holy man joined them as husband and wife.

Stripping out of the armor she wore today, she smoothed a hand over the vivid blossom that still resided between her legs. There her tattooing of the experienced whore had ended.

A fierce pirate captain, Fu had defied his men, taken her aboard his ship, and sailed her away from a life of prostitution. A brutal fighter by day, he turned into a gentle lover by night. Telling her once he saw her, he couldn't bear the thought of another man's hands upon her. She was his, as if she were made for his eyes alone. The universe had created her for him. He treated her with nothing but gentleness, care, and respect.

When he finally took Jun into his bed, he worshipped her body and touched her soul. He stopped her the moment she tried to use her training from the brothel to please him. Kept her from taking him into her mouth after she'd brazenly and submissively knelt before him. He'd taken her by the arms and lifted her to her feet. "You are not my whore, Jun, you are my wife." His reverence for her and loving kindness laid siege to her heart, and she surrendered.

Together they became an unstoppable pair. Jian Fu built his fleet and ruled much of the South China Seas. But a short three years later, during a battle with a Dutch frigate, she lost him as a cannonball nearly cut him in two.

She held him while he died, with his blood forever staining her memory. He made Jun promise she would never allow herself to return to her former life. His last wish was for her to fight and realize their dreams of a great pirate empire. Jian Jun had done just that.

Defying convention, and rules of proper succession, Jun claimed Fu's fleet the day she marched into the meeting of his commanders wearing armor four sizes too large. Perhaps they had been stunned, or perhaps they had humored her out of respect for their fallen captain, but she had taken up the reins of Fu's domain, and here some eight years later, had built upon the strength of their dynasty to command a fleet of close to one thousand ships. More than sixty thousand men, women, and children worked for Jun. Fought for her. Stole and seized for her.

She was rich beyond measure, and provided an abundant life for all who served under her. Generous when moved, yet ruthless when needed. Jun carried on her husband's position as well as his unbending rules.

Standing naked before her looking glass, she couldn't help the pain of loss that still sliced through her when she thought of him. After all these years, the bite of that blade had lost its fiery edge, but she missed Fu terribly. There had been no one since, although many had tried to win her affection. None had succeeded. All had left her cold.

She was not blind to their ambitions. It was more power and might that attracted them than her womanly promise. Jun refused them all. Even Peng, although his attentions were proclaimed to be out of honest caring and admiration. She was not interested. After all these years in solitude, she had earned her title of the Ice Empress.

Jun wrapped herself in a robe of brilliant red silk and moved outside her rooms to the private gardens beyond. High walls protected the space and created a sanctuary of thick-trunked palm trees, beautiful flowering plants of every color, and restive pools of clear water. Bright koi swam in lazy curls between the cool plates of the lily pads. Comfortable cushions were scattered throughout. A tray of fruits sat waiting. She lifted a firm mandarin orange and lifted it to her nose to breathe in its sweet citrus scent.

It was then she saw her. Her maidservant, Ting's small daughter, Pei Qi was tucked between two overflowing planters. No more than five, she was filling her cheeks with ripe gooseberries, sneaking furtive glances behind her as she popped each pearl of fruit into her mouth. Jun tipped her head and cleared her throat, but it was Ting's approach, which ended up driving the child straight into Jun's arms.

"I've caught you." Jun held her.

The girl jumped back, dropping the pale green cluster to the ground and stared up at Jun with wide dark eyes. Ting was of pure Chinese descent as was Jun, but her daughter's father was a westerner who now served on one of Jun's ships. Their union in marriage had produced the most beautiful child with her mother's dark locks and eyes and honeyed skin, but with the curl of her father's hair and the round shape of his European eyes.

Many set in the ancient ways and beliefs shunned Qi's mixed heritage, and it was believed that the unnatural combination of races was the cause of the child's simple nature. Qi behaved more like a mischievous pet than a typical child. Hiding in the shadows. Making small squeaks and whines. Doctors told Ting it was doubtful Qi would ever progress mentally like a normal child. It was considered her punishment. Many were cruel in their comments and actions against both mother and daughter. It was one of the reasons Jun had taken Ting on as her personal servant and given them both the protection and shelter of that position.

"You little thief." Ting grabbed at the child's arm, but she only managed to slip from her mother's grasp and scuttle beneath a hibiscus bush and out of reach. "I'm so sorry Mistress Jian. She doesn't understand what she does."

"It's fine. Gooseberries are her favorite."

"And she will eat them until she gets sick, even though I tell her to stop. She doesn't listen." Ting shot a worried glance back at her daughter.

"She's still a babe." Jun picked up the discarded fruit and handed it back to Ting. "Qi is determined to learn some lessons the hard way."

"I'm afraid she won't ever learn them." Ting lowered her gaze.

"Perhaps not, but she has a gentle heart behind those soulful eyes, and two parents who love her. It is more than most."

"Yes, Mistress. It seems I am forever grateful for your patience with her."

"Qi is a lovely blessing for me. She is like this garden. A tiny secret oasis hidden within the great pressures of my station. I can't imagine what my life would be without either of them."

For a brief, fanciful moment, Jian Jun gave in to thoughts of that simpler life of childlike innocence. She rubbed at where her armor straps chafed at her skin. No, the future was etched upon her skin, like the lotus decorating her sex.

Her fate was permanent.

Chapter 3

Sailing the *Scarlet Night* northeast from Madagascar, Will made the decision to keep the *Night* far to the south of Seychelles. Held by the French, it would be almost as dangerous as pulling into Portsmouth harbor. The French and English weren't what you would call allies, and with the hefty price upon all their heads, particularly his and Tupper's, it would take little encouragement from the French to turn them over for the sizable reward offered for their capture.

In Tupper's cabin, Will pored over the maps and charts spread out before him. Perhaps a quick stop in the southernmost Maldives. He circled the area with a fingertip and tapped the spot. There appeared to be a peaceful lagoon within the lowermost atoll. Four channels would bring them safely through the scattering of small islands if the maps were accurate. They could rest a while in those warm turquoise waters and gather fresh native fruits and fish. Perhaps trade with the locals for the rest of their supplies. Will wanted them fully prepared. The last leg of their journey wouldn't be easy even if they knew these waters.

Will traced his finger along their proposed course bringing them down the Malacca Strait and directly into Singapore harbor. According to all Will had learned on their voyage, the strait was a pirate's dream…or a captain's nightmare. Hundreds of islands dotted the wide channel. Perfect places to hide and wait for a choice ship to attack. The *Scarlet's* crew would be on high alert for days. And, if they managed to skirt the constant threat of a pirate strike, there were miles of treacherous coral reefs to navigate that could easily rip into the hull and strip the bottom clean off a ship. Too many vessels had found their watery ends there for one reason or the other.

They were crazy to think they could make it through unscathed. The men had already voiced their concerns, according to Griffin, but this was

Will's decision. It was the fastest way to get Tupper to China and to the medicines necessary to save her life, and he'd be damned if the grumbles of a few men would stop him.

As if his thought conjured her, Tupper entered her quarters. Will's jaw tightened at the sight of her. His fingers curled around the handle of the dirk lying near him on the desk. If only he could fight her battle with pistol and sword. Frustration surged through him. She'd lost too much weight. Her clothing now hung on her frame. The day's sun had done its best to brighten her cheeks from the paleness she'd worn these last few weeks.

'Beautiful day on deck. Go topside. Get away from that desk.' She gestured toward the door.

Will pointed to the work before him. *'Logs. Charts.'*

Tupper swept her forehead to sign, *'Forget them.'*

He shook his head and pulled the current log from its protected chest. All the ship's ledgers were kept safe in their ornately carved, cork-lined box. Well, perhaps not all. A shelf of ship's logs dating back more than thirty years filled the glass-fronted bookcase in the corner of the chamber. Only two volumes from Will's short tenure as captain currently held the place of honor in their nest of cork. The chest had been Gavin's addition to the efficient workings of his office. The name of the ship was beautifully carved into the cover along with an artist's rendition of the *Scarlet Night* in battle.

Tupper pulled over a short stool and sat to the side of the wide oak desk. Running a finger over the engraved top of the familiar box, she gave a wistful grin. *'Fine, but take a break for a minute.'* Tupper signed and held his gaze, a familiar look of determination setting her features. He knew that look and inwardly groaned. She still held a bit of her edge. Once Tupper had her mind made up about something…

He dropped his quill back into the secured inkpot and waved his hand, palm up, *'What?'*

Tupper set her chin. *'I want to talk to you, and I don't want you to stop me.'*

He'd been right to groan. Will braced himself. *'When have I ever been able to stop you?'*

'Never.' A smile tugged at the corner of her mouth before her gaze fell to the floor. She rubbed her palms together and took a long moment before taking off her ring and placing it before him on the desk. She massaged her finger where the evidence of the gold oval signet ring remained. The crease of the band and the whiteness of the skin beneath lay in sharp contrast to her tanned finger. Will couldn't recall ever seeing her without her treasured ring until now.

He picked it up and ran the pad of his thumb over the ornate "A" with a fine, small pearl caught in the sweep of the initial gracing the face of the piece. The "A" stood for Alice. Tupper's given name. The ring had been given to her as a gift from her best friend before she left England more than thirty years ago.

Will lifted his gaze to hers in question. *'Need it polished?'*

'I want you to have it.'

He didn't need to be a fine scholar to figure out what she was doing. He shoved the ring across the surface of the desk back toward her, shaking his head.

Tupper stopped him by covering his hand with hers and pushing back. She then tapped the side of her index finger against her opposite palm. *'Don't argue with me.'* She set her jaw before continuing. Her hands quickly speaking to him in the signing language they had both used to communicate all these years. *'I've only lied once to you in your lifetime. To protect you. But you're a grown man and a good captain, and I'm not about to lie to you now. We both know the truth. I'm on my way out of this damn life, and I want you to have this before I go.'* She pointed back to the ring. *'It's all I own that's truly mine. Didn't steal it. Didn't barter for it. Didn't kill for it...well, that's not quite true, but it was only 'cause the bastard stole it from me an' I was gettin' it back.'* She wiped at the air with her hand as if disregarding her last bit of ramble before giving Will a stern look. *'How many times can I cheat death and get away with it? Won't be so lucky as to escape this time.'*

'Ye're not giving up yet.' He pointed to the chart before signing, *'Less than two weeks before we dock in China. Their doctors are the best there be.'*

'Take the ring anyway. For safekeeping. Damn thing keeps slipping off my scrawny finger.' She lifted his hand and pushed it securely onto his right pinky before giving his hand a squeeze. He considered the brightness of the gold against the darkness of his skin. The weight of it felt odd upon his hand... Its weight felt heavy on his shoulders as well.

* * * *

More than a week later, the *Scarlet Night* fought strange winds and cross currents as they dodged the many islands found within the famed Malacca Strait. They'd been fortunate up to this point to keep their distance from other ships. Even the sleek junks with their bright flags flying from their masts to appease the dragons and their odd shell-shaped, battened sails. The *Night's* speed together with the honeycomb of islands along the strait had served them well.

The men would have preferred to battle and add to their wealth, but Will couldn't risk possible damage to the *Scarlet Night* slowing their progress. Looking out past the bowsprit he only hoped for swift, calm seas ahead.

Turning back to scan the length of the *Night*, a large, yellow alert flag with lead balls sewn into its hems hit the deck mid ship. Will's gaze shot to the crow's nest where the man there also yanked on the bell cord in alarm before pointing sharply toward the west. Will grabbed for his spyglass, but one glance told him he didn't need it. A fist twisted in his gut.

Dark ominous clouds lined the horizon. Will knew exactly what headed their way. In these waters, quick strange storms rose up unexpectedly, bringing strong thirty to forty knot winds and intense downpours. Hellish storms, but fast moving. Still they were in for a wild ride.

Griffin joined Will on the port rail. *'Sumatran?'* He finger spelled the word. Will nodded. *'Looks to be. Lash everything down. Drop every sail. We'll ride it out.'* He moved to the upper deck and took command of the ship's thick oak wheel from Simon Hills, the helmsman. Without Griffin to translate, Will himself would move them far enough away from the coastline and into deeper, safer water. There was no telling how the storm would toss them about and he didn't want to run the risk of catching the *Night* on a reef.

Surveying the length of the ship once more, Will watched each of his orders carried out with swift and practiced precision. Every man down to the lowest powder monkey executed their duty flawlessly. A finer crew didn't sail these waters or any other.

Men raced into the rigging and secured each sail on the *Scarlet's* three masts. As the winds began to lift the heavy ropes of Will's hair, anything that could move on deck was secured. Barrels were lashed to masts and rails. Cannon locks checked. Lines tightened.

The sky overhead turned menacing, but Will was confident they were ready for the tempest heading their way. Tupper battled against the growing winds to join him at the helm. She gripped the arm of his shirt to steady herself. He couldn't let go of the wheel to order her below. Instead, he jerked his chin in that direction. To his surprise, she moved off without arguing, stopping only once to say something to Griffin.

Soon wind and driving rain plastered Will's shirt to his chest and dripped from his thick hair. He and Griffin combined their strength to hold tight to the *Night's* wheel as the ship was buffered and battered by the storm. Great waves crashed over the bow. The sea around them frothed and foamed as if it boiled.

After hours of fighting, the storm showed none of the familiar signs of passing. In fact, as the darkness of night blackened the skies around them, it only grew worse. This wasn't a common Sumatran.

They had sailed straight into a blinding, bloody hurricane.

Seawater and rain stung at Will's eyes and filled his mouth and nose. Great bolts of lightning split the sky and gave an eerie, hellish vision to the typhoon that engulfed them. His muscles burned and strained with the effort of keeping the *Scarlet Night* from being swamped in the ferocious seas. In the darkness, Will could no longer distinguish the coastline. With each flash of lightning, he struggled to find the shore, certain at any moment he would run them aground.

The sky lit once more with branched jagged swords of light. It was then he saw her. Tupper. Braced in the bow of the ship, clutching the rigging. Her clothing plastered to her thin body. Her boots slipping with each buck of the ship while she clung on through the beating of the waves over the rails. Icy fingers clawed at Will's heart. Any minute she'd be washed overboard.

Will pounded on Griffin's back, praying the man would know he was leaving him to battle alone. He released his death grip upon the pegs of the wheel and moved by sheer force of will and blind luck down the pitching ladderway to the rolling deck below. A vicious wave shoved the ship to starboard and slammed him into the portside rail. Will struggled to grab for any hold in the darkness. He had to get to Tupper before it was too late.

The next flash of lightning revealed her again. Somehow in the middle of these churning seas, Tupper had managed to climb higher in the ropes toward the bowsprit. She shook her fist at the sky. Mouth open, the tendons in her neck strained against a fervent scream Will could only see. Who was she railing at? The storm? The sea? God, Himself? Will pushed past the roil of his stomach and fought to reach her.

It was then the *Scarlet Night* met her final shot. In the obscurity of the black night, the ship struck something with such force, Will was thrown head-first into the foaming water. He hit the angry waves like a fist. The cold shock dragging him down, tossing and rolling his body until he couldn't distinguish up from down. The sea was quick to fill his boots and pull him toward his certain death. Down he went. His lungs soon burning with the urgent need for air.

Will fought with every shred of his being. Struggling, he pulled free of his boots and kicked in the only direction that could be up. How far to the surface? Surely his lungs would burst before he reached it. Instinct and survival pushed him past the point of surrender, but he could feel the tempting pull of death calling him into her cold embrace. If he just stopped struggling...

His arm hit air as he broke the surface and gasped in a breath. Waves continued to crash over him and toss him about as he fought to stay alive. Where was the *Night*? Tupper? Had she been thrown from the decks as well? He had to find his way back to her.

Lightning pierced the black once more. Will spun about in a mad search before the dark could capture him again. Against the storm, he could barely make out the silhouette of the *Scarlet Night*'s once-proud masts pitched at a deadly angle. The ship was going down. They'd come in too close and she'd wrecked upon the reef. In the blackness of the storm, he pushed toward the wreck. Adrenaline pulsing through his limbs. The beating of the waves upon the coral would tear her apart. All would be lost. He had to reach them.

Through the dark, he battled against the relentless waves that shoved him with a mighty hand beneath the rolling surface. Sharp fingers of coral tore at his leg; the pounding of each surge beat him back. In the next slice of light, Will could no longer see her. Terror clawed at his gut. Where was the ship? Could the *Scarlet Night* truly be gone? No, he must be turned around. Desperation turned to panic as he continued to flounder in the punishing seas.

Will made another frantic attempt to reach the area where he had last seen the *Night*, but the fight of the waves was stronger than he was. It filled his belly with seawater and blinded him in the silent hell storm that continued to flood over him and drag him under until he couldn't fight it anymore. Death's sweet call bid to him once again. The battle lost.

Chapter 4

Jun went over the reports of losses due to the storm that moved over them through the night. She'd lost four ships of her own to the bite of the reefs and understood there was evidence of other wrecks washing up along the eastern coast of the island.

Fortunately, when her husband had built his grand palace, he had the sense to situate it so it rarely felt the brunt of the unpredictable weather along this end of the Strait. Of the two islands Pandang and Salahnama, known to all in this area as The Brothers, Pandang was the most sheltered of the two.

Last night's gales had been particularly fierce, however. Many of her people were busy at work cleaning up the damage to their properties, the wide crescent beach that graced the southern shore, and her own precious garden. Peng himself was overseeing the rebuilding of two of the northern docks weakened by the high seas.

Ke Zhao, one of her lieutenants, pushed into the great hall. He stopped before her, bowed in respect, and waited to speak.

"What is it?"

The man lifted his gaze to hers. "I am in search of General Chou Peng, Mistress."

Jun rolled the parchment in her hands. "He is busy seeing to other matters. What did you need to see him about?"

"A man, Mistress. A stranger. My men found him at the water's edge this morning."

"He must have come from one of the lost ships. Is he dead?"

"No. He was unconscious at first, but has come around."

Jun set the parchment aside and stood. "What vessel did he travel upon? Was he armed? Sent by our enemies? Have you questioned him?"

Ke Zhao nodded. "We have, but he stubbornly refused to respond.

He is unarmed; however, when we put restraints on him, he reacted with extreme violence. As if he were suddenly a caged beast, and yet still he says nothing. I thought it best to seek the general's counsel."

"Bring him to me."

The man faltered. "But, Mistress…"

Jun planted her hands on her hips. "I said, bring him to me. If he is a stranger, as you say, he will not understand your tongue. I will speak to him. I trust your men can keep him under control?"

"Yes, of course Mistress, but…" He gripped at the belt holding his sword. His fingers worried the leather.

Jun notched her chin and pulled a short dagger from the top of her boot. "Bring him to me…unless you've grown overly fond of your ears and would like them removed."

Ke's eyes widened before he took a single step back and gave her a sharp bow. "As you wish."

A short time later, Ke Zhao returned. Behind him, two of his men struggled to drag a large, dark man between them. He was wet and covered with a fine film of sand, which made his rich skin almost shimmer in the room's lantern light. Thick dark hanks of twisted hair hung past his broad shoulders. Strong arms flexed and bunched as he fought against his iron restraints. He was unshod, the remnants of his shirt clung in strips to the planes of his chest, and one torn leg of his pants revealed angry scrapes along his shin. An ugly gash over one eyebrow wept dark blood down the side of his face.

The men released him, and forced him to his knees before her. Jun could see where his wrists were worn raw by his fight against his bounds. Ke Zhao had told the truth. The man's reaction at being restrained was curious indeed.

Jun spoke to him in English. "If you tell me your name and promise to act in a civilized manner, I will see your shackles removed."

When he didn't respond, didn't so much as move, Zhao grabbed him by the back of his hair and forced his head up. Eyes the color of the finest topaz glared at her beneath dark brows. Their stunning intensity caused a catch in her breath. It was as if he could see clear to her soul.

She composed herself and asked once more in clear English, "I ask you again, what is your name?" Still the man remained silent. His only movement was to lower his gaze to watch her mouth as she spoke. Jun was clever enough to know a handful of other languages and repeated the question in all of them with the same lack of response from the handsome stranger.

Lieutenant Ke struck the man and screamed for him to answer before pulling his dagger and holding it to the man's throat. At that same moment, Chou Peng and his men burst into the great hall shouting at the disgrace and dishonor of dragging a prisoner into Jun's presence. Ke Zhao lowered his weapon and began hastily explaining the scene amidst Peng's thunderous rant.

It was in the booming chaos of the heated exchange between the two men when Jun noticed something more about the man kneeling before her. A quick glance around the room confirmed that all eyes were on Peng, and yet the prisoner acted as if nothing was happening behind him.

"Stop, all of you." Jun ordered pulling one of her swords. Why must some men behave like barbarians? She swung the honed blade. "I said, stop!"

"Take this man away from here this instant," bellowed Peng.

"No." Jun stepped off the dais and approached the man. "There is something curious. Stand behind him for a moment." When Peng did so, she continued. "Clap your hands together."

"What…?"

"Do as I say. Sharply. Twice."

Peng clapped his hands. The man held her gaze and never blinked. "Ke, stay where you are and drop your weapon to the stones." The man followed her order. When the iron hilt of his knife hit the tiled floor the man didn't so much as twitch. Jun confirmed her suspicions.

"What are you thinking?" Peng returned to Jun's side and narrowed his eyes at the man before them.

"I believe our prisoner is not rebelliously defying our requests. Or that he speaks some mysterious foreign tongue. It is my thinking this man is deaf."

As if to confirm it for himself, Peng moved behind the man once more, pulled his own dagger from its sheath, and dropped it with a loud clatter.

Jun stood before the unflinching prisoner. "Release him."

Peng protested. "Just because he is without hearing doesn't mean he isn't a danger to you."

Jun sheathed her weapon. "I'll take my chances."

The man stood to his full imposing height the moment the shackles left his wrists. Jun had to tip her chin to continue to hold his gaze. Around her weapons were quickly drawn, but she held up her hand to stop any intrusion from her men.

"Someone bring me a bit of charcoal from the fire." She retrieved the parchment scroll she'd been reviewing earlier and tore a piece away from its edge. When she returned to the silent man, she pointed to the middle of her chest before scrawling *Jun* with that small bit of charcoal. Jun repeated the motion of pointing to her chest, then pointing to her name. Next, she looked expectantly to him in question, pointed to the center of his broad chest and held out the parchment.

He reached out to pluck the charcoal from her stained fingers and taking the parchment, he braced it on one strong thigh before writing in bold block letters, *Captain William Quinn.*

* * * *

Will mimicked what the woman standing before him had done. He pointed to his chest and back to the parchment before turning the scrap over and writing, *My ship the* Scarlet Night *wrecked on the reef. Have you found any other survivors?* Every cell in his body, his head, and his gut ached in protest. It was a true struggle to stand. His lungs hurt to breathe, but it was a damn sight better than not being able to breathe at all. Somehow the sea had thrown him up last night and spared him. Only fitting that he had thrown up half the sea, as well, as his body rejected the gallon of seawater in his belly and lungs. But what of the others? There had to be others who washed ashore with him. He pushed a finger at what he'd written.

The beautiful Chinese woman named Jun met his gaze briefly before speaking to the others. Will turned to read their faces as they responded. His heart, like his beloved *Scarlet Night*, sank deeper as each man shook his head and looked in question to the next.

He closed his eyes to the pain that razored through him. His ship, his crew, Tupper...all lost? Will opened his eyes with a start to check his hand. A thin ray of relief pierced the darkness. Tupper's ring still remained tightly bound to his finger. Its ornate "A" winking brightly. He moved to run his thumb over the letter when he noticed the pearl was gone. The small point of perfect white that had forever graced the face of her precious ring... It had been reclaimed by the sea.

Will's right knee buckled under a wave of grief fiercer than those he survived through the storm. The threat of tears burned the backs of his eyes. He covered them with his hand and fought to remain standing.

Anger surged through him. No! This cannot be! Why? Dear God, why? Why should he be spared to carry the weight of this anguish alone? What possible reason could there be for him to have lived when the rest had died?

He wouldn't give up hope that the others could have survived. Will raked his hand down his face. Sand and salt still coated his skin. An odd man came to join the scimitar-swinging woman standing before him. They appeared to be arguing, and she was clearly winning. Her unworthy opponent was dressed in purple from head to toe. He resembled a skinny, bearded grape. So gaunt, his chin could have sliced cheese. In true Chinese style, the front of his head was shaved bald, leaving a long sharp pigtail to trail down his back. He was obviously a man of some power unlike these other bastards who split his forehead before they shackled him and dragged him from the beach. Now he'd have a matching scar to the one those British curs gave him when they'd first arrested him.

Will took a longer look at the woman. Clad in thick, black leather armor and a gold-trimmed breast plate that molded perfectly to each curve of her body, it was obvious she commanded a great deal of authority. The ornate headdress she wore could have easily been a crown. A queen with matching gold-hilted scimitars and boots that ended high on her thighs. Past the harsh edges of her uniform and the mighty swing of her sword, however, her striking beauty could not be denied. Smooth skin the color of rich cream held a soft blush high along her cheeks. Her full lips a shade of pink slightly darker, and the almond shape of her eyes darkened with kohl only added to her exotic appeal.

Wait a minute. His waterlogged mind took a moment to put all the pieces together. *Dammit.* Will was quick to turn over the parchment he still held. *Jun.* She'd written that her name was Jun. As in *Jian* Jun? Empress of the Dragon's Fire Fleet? Most powerful, deadly pirate to ever sail the South China Seas? It had to be her. How many other commanding, goddess-like Juns could there be? She was legendary. Stories of her might and brutality reached far and wide on this side of the world and even beyond her fleet's reach. *Bloody hell.*

She turned those stunning eyes to his once more. Will held up the parchment, tapped at her name before adding *Jian.* He looked back to her in question. She narrowed her eyes and slipped her hand over the hilt of her sword before giving him the smallest nod.

Son of a bitch. He was in the presence of a bloody goddess. And a gorgeous one at that. Will straightened his bruised and battered body to its full height before bending at the waist and giving her a deep bow of respect. Rising, he noticed it was the skinny grape's turn to narrow his eyes in mistrust.

Chapter 5

Peng barked to his men, "Take him away."

Jun halted them. "No. He is not our prisoner."

Peng held up a hand to stop his men. The muscle in his jaw tightened before he snarled his objection to her in English once more. "He knows your name. Who you are. I say we restrain the man again and hold him until we can find out more about him."

"That is my decision to make. So he knows of me. That is not surprising, and it is not a reason to treat him as a prisoner. He has greeted me with respect."

"I don't trust him." Peng scowled.

"You trust no one." Jun swept her hand in the captain's direction. "Look at him. He can barely stand. He is certainly no threat." Jun did another slow sweep of his body. Few around her matched him in height alone. His skin was the color of strong tea. It was the odd lightness of his eyes that continued to capture her. She wanted to test the heavy texture of his hair. Everything about him intrigued her.

Jun continued. "The man has been through a horrible ordeal. He reads and writes English, which means he's a westerner. Aren't you curious how he and his ship made the journey here? Which route they took? Need I remind you, we are seeking to answer the mystery of those routes to broaden the fleet's reach? He may have useful information we can use. I doubt he will be inclined to tell us if we treat him with such hostilities."

Peng moved closer and lowered his voice. "I mean not to question your authority, but as your general it is my duty to protect you."

Jun raised her chin and glared at him. "When have I ever needed your protection? I am more than capable of protecting myself." She indicated the captain. "He is surrounded on all sides by my people. Wounded, exhausted, and unarmed. How much of a danger do you believe he is?" Jun gave Peng an impatient glance. "And why do you insist on whispering before a deaf man?"

Peng shot the captain a suspicious look. "His inability to hear could be a clever ruse."

"Nonsense." To her servants she called, "Send for my physician. Ting, prepare a room, a bath, and a meal for our guest. See if you can find him something suitable to wear." She turned back to Peng. "I want you to send a dozen men to comb the shoreline. See if you can find any evidence of the ship called the *Scarlet Night*. Perhaps there are more of his crew in need of our help."

The look in Peng's eyes spoke of his smoldering anger. It wasn't the first time his actions forced her to override his authority, but he had the good sense not to act on such fury. At least, not in her presence. First mate or not, he was as any other under her command. Her word was final and the law, and he understood the deadly consequences of disobedience.

She turned away from him. "You have your orders. You are dismissed."

Peng stiffened with indignance beside her. He stepped before her, gathering his dignity and bowed before turning back, collecting his men with a shout, and leaving the great hall.

Ting approached to usher Captain Quinn away. Jun wished she had asked for a larger piece of coal so could tell him all was well, and that they were going to care for him. Communication was going to be a challenge between them. All she could do was put a gentle hand on his arm and give him a small smile before handing him over to Ting. She hoped he would gather her meaning. As Ting pulled him away, Jun added one more request. "While the doctor sees to him, please gather proper writing things and put them in his room, quill, ink, parchment. We'll need those as well."

A short time later, her personal physician, Yeh Tien-shih, met with her. "How is Captain Quinn?" Her words came in a rush. She hadn't been able to think of much else save the handsome stranger since he landed at her feet.

"Beaten. Bruised. Weak, but otherwise fit. His lungs sound clear, but it is no surprise, his breathing continues to labor some. I do believe his lack of hearing is absolute. He is a captain, you say? I've never heard of a deaf man commanding a ship. Quite remarkable even for a merchant. In any case, I've cleaned the wound on his forehead and stitched it closed. I wanted to perform acupuncture to ease his discomfort, but he resisted. Strongly. His other wounds appear minor. Healing salve is all that is needed. And rest. I've given him a strong herbal tincture. He should sleep soundly for hours."

"Thank you, doctor." Jun attempted to return to her work, although concentrating on anything other than her growing questions regarding the captain continued to prove challenging. Curiosity could be a great curse at times, and patience was clearly not one of her virtues.

Yeh Tien-shih moved to leave, and paused. "I did discover something most disturbing when I examined Captain Quinn. A past injury to be sure. Nothing that will affect his recovery, but he's suffered a severe wounding."

Jun lifted her gaze. "Oh?"

The doctor frowned. "The man's body bears several battle signs I wouldn't consider typical for a simple seaman. A warrior perhaps? Scars from blades and fists mark him. He also carries distinct marks of being shot in the back. Twice. A true miracle in their positioning. Another fraction one side or another, and they would have killed him. Or crippled him, at the very least. He's lucky to be alive."

"A coward's assault to shoot a man in the back. More so a deaf man." She wondered how it happened. Jun added the question to the long list of curiosities regarding Captain Quinn and his story. "Seems death has no need for him."

"Seems so." Yeh inclined his head. "I will continue with his care, but I feel a few days of rest and healthy food will be the best medicine for him. He's young, virile. He'll be strong again in no time."

For the rest of the day, Jun found every possible excuse to walk the passageways through the east wing of the palace until she met Ting coming from the captain's sleeping chamber carrying a tray of food and other burdens.

"Mistress?"

"There you are." Jun's mind scrambled for a plausible lie. "Qi has been searching for you." Guilt strained her conscience. She was quick to ease any shame her words might inflict. "I fear I've distracted you from your regular duties today. I didn't imagine my requests would keep you here so long."

Ting lowered her gaze to the tray. "This is the second time I've been back. He didn't touch any of the fish stew I brought to him earlier. I only just left him a bit of rice and tea if he changes his mind in the night."

"Trust you to be so efficient. You're kindhearted. I'm sure by tomorrow his appetite will have returned. Is he sleeping?" Jun glanced back at his door. The image of him stretched out along his bed slipped through her imaginings.

"Yes, mistress."

Jun studied the pale slide of paper wall. Artists had painted the panels in pale lovely scenes of the surrounding mountains and seas. So different from her own thick walls of stone and wood. A fortress compared to the captain's penetrable room.

"The doctor believes he will be well in a few days. It is good he is resting."

"There is one other matter." Ting set the food tray at her feet and pulled a garment from under one arm and held it out for Jun to see.

"This is much too small. He is a grand man…wide shoulders, long legs. I've not found garments to fit him."

Jun fingered the garments. The image of Captain Quinn's broad chest made her smile. "Did you save what was left of the clothing he was wearing?"

"Yes, mistress."

"Take them to my dressmakers. Tell them I will need a proper changshan for a man that size by morning."

Ting inclined her head. "At once, mistress, but first I must tend to you. I have called for your evening meal, and will come heat water for your bath."

Jun shook her head and touched Ting's arm. "No, you have done enough of my bidding today. I can carry my own water."

"But it is my honored duty." Ting bowed again.

"Your duty is to see to my wishes, and you have served me well. It is my next wish that after you carry my message to the tailors, you spend the rest of your day with your daughter."

"But, mistress…"

"I am capable of undressing myself and combing my own hair. Go." She looked back toward the paper wall. "Who knows what the new day will bring. I will need you fresh and bright come morning."

A small smile tipped Ting's mouth. "I will come early. Will bring the changshan for the stranger as soon as it is ready."

Stranger. Was he still considered a stranger when Jun had spent every hour since he was dropped at her feet wondering about him? Her insatiable desire to discover everything continued to surprise her. She had come to learn more about him in these last few hours than most of the men under her command. Nay, he was not truly a stranger anymore.

Jun lifted the tray Ting had placed on the floor and handed it back to her. Glancing back at the fragile sliding entrance to his room, she corrected her. "His name is Captain Quinn."

* * * *

The halls were quiet. The palace was sleeping. Jun had stripped out of her cage of steel and leather armor, and into a lavish embroidered robe of the palest blue. Face scrubbed and hair combed, she found herself still consumed with thoughts of her guest. The doctor said he would be asleep for hours. Perhaps she should have asked for a bit of his strong tincture for herself.

Sleep had always been an elusive thing for her. Tonight was no exception but for the addition of the good captain. She couldn't stop thinking about him. Wondering about him and his history, and how he came to be a captain. Even Yeh Tien-shih had agreed his inability to hear would make his rank surprising. He must be an extraordinary man.

Or, he was lying.

Surprisingly, he knew of her even being from the west. It would have pleased her late husband to know how after his death she had continued to build upon his dream of a fleet so vast and infamous, the whole world would know of them and tremble in fear at their name.

Jun picked up her pipa, and plucked a few notes from its twisted silk strings before silencing the instrument with a frustrated slap of her hand. The escape of music usually relaxed her, but not this night. She set the lute aside and moved to her desk as the day's ledgers still needed her attention. Work would fill her long empty hours as it had for so many years. She raised the flame on her lamp and opened the tall, columned pages, but the figures soon blurred and swam beneath her gaze as her mind drifted once again to the unusual man with the topaz eyes. Slamming the ledger closed, she rose, and stepped out into her garden.

The slight pale curve of a fingernail moon carved through a night sky rich with stars. Sweet smells and the gentle trickle of water into the ponds would surely lull her to sleep. It wouldn't be the first time she found her rest between the flowers. Jun curled up on one of the wide pillows tucked between the plantings and closed her eyes.

Deep, steady breaths. She remembered when she was a small child. Younger than Qi. When her mother would rock her in her arms on nights such as these and tell her to close her eyes.

"Imagine a great tall tree with a thick twisted trunk and limbs that stretch high into the night's sky, In that tree there lived a small bright bird with wings the color of fire. Her name was Jun. Each day she would play within the cool shelter of that tall magnificent tree preening her feathers and singing beautiful songs."

Jun would snuggle closer, picturing herself with long wings of red and gold, hopping among the branches. Closing her eyes, Jun could still smell the soap her mother used to scrub their clothing.

"Each night while the other birds slept, Jun would climb to the very top of the tree. You see, it was her chore each night to count the leaves."

"But, mother, there are too many leaves. She'll never be able to count them all."

Jun recalled her mother's patient voice. *"Hush child. She doesn't need to count them all. Just the ones that help bring you to your sleep."*

Jun pulled in a sweet breath of warm night air and began to count the cool green leaves in her mind's eye. But soon, thoughts of the great tall tree returned her musings to the great tall Captain Quinn. The twisted trunk reminded her of the odd twists of his hair. Forget the leaves. Jun sat and tightened the thin robe around her. There were too many questions to count, and she longed to know the answer to each one.

She was on her feet and padding silently toward his sleeping chamber before sanity could rein her in once more. Jun looked behind her, and down the hall, ensuring she was not observed. Slowly she slid the ornate panel open only enough to slip through before closing it behind her. Standing for a moment next to a braided bamboo plant close to the door, Jun waited for the erratic beating of her heart to slow.

The room's lantern still burned low on a short table close to the room's sleeping k'ang, casting a warm yellowed glow over its occupant's features. It caught the smooth curve of his lips, pale in comparison with the raspy appearance of new beard. The cut of his cheekbones, and the noble slope of his nose. His bare chest rose and fell in deep full breaths. A sheet covered him from his waist to his feet, both of which reached well past the end of the bed.

With great care not to make a single sound, she tiptoed closer, before realizing how ridiculous she was being. He couldn't hear her. She could march into the room clanging cymbals and beating on drums and wouldn't wake him.

Jun shook her head at her foolishness. The whole scene was foolish. Why was she here? She should leave at once and cease this madness. But Jun didn't leave. Couldn't. She peeked over her shoulder again. Nervousness bubbled up in her chest. If anyone were to catch her in this man's room, how would she explain herself? Curiosity? Snooping?

She moved to the table. The rice, tea and bit of fruit Ting had left appeared untouched. Writing instruments lay nearby just as she had instructed. Jun lifted the corked bottle of tincture the doctor had said he left. Pulling the cork, she sniffed at the contents. The sharp smell of fermented herbs stung her nose. She pushed it aside with a grimace.

Jun glanced over at the sleeping man once more, taking a measure of guilty pleasure in studying his strong features and lower to the planes of his muscled chest. Her gaze traveled over the ridges of his abdomen as a ridiculous desire to see all of him flushed through her. What was wrong with her? She was surrounded by men. Thousands of them. This man was no different. But even as the thought materialized, she knew it to be a lie.

He was different, and not just because he was deaf. He was a riddle and a mystery. His size, the color of his skin, the dark bristle shadowing his handsome jaw, all made him unique and unusual. And his hair. Her fingers itched to test the weight and feel of it.

Before she could help herself, Jun reached out and lifted one of the long twisted hanks of hair that covered his head. It wasn't as heavy as it looked. And not coarse at all. She'd never seen another man weave his hair quite that way. It couldn't occur naturally, could it? How?

A swift hand grabbed hold of her wrist. Jun caught her startled scream by slapping her other hand over her mouth. Shaded golden eyes glared at her beneath dark brows.

Jun was able to pull out of his grasp and back up several paces as Captain Quinn rose and swung his legs over the side of his bed. The k'ang's sheet covering him barely covered him any longer. Jun couldn't take her eyes away from the length of strong thigh peeking out beneath the inadequate sheet.

She shook her head, dragged her eyes away from the seductive sight of him forever etched in her mind, and held her hands up in surrender. "I'm so sorry. I didn't mean to wake you. I don't know what came over me. I…" She stopped, and lowered her hands. "You…have no idea what I'm saying, do you? I could be telling you I plan to kill you, cook you, and eat you for my breakfast and it wouldn't make one bit of difference. I could tell you what a stunning picture you make sitting there, and how I've done nothing since we met but wonder about you."

An intriguing thought ran through her mind at the same time her body reacted to the sheer presence of him in such close quarters. It had been so long since any man had stirred even the slightest interest in her. The flood of sensation made her tremble. Her nipples tightened to hardened points beneath the silk of her robe. "In fact, I could talk to you about anything at all. Tell you all my secrets. Confess anything I wanted. Tell you that right this moment I would like to have you stand before me naked and proud before kneeling and pledging yourself to me. Giving yourself to me."

To her utter shock, he stood.

Jun's heart threatened to punch its way out of her chest. A rush of forbidden pleasure dampened her sex. Had he not wrapped the sheet around his waist, she might have fainted. So much for her bravado.

Had he heard her all along? Heat rushed to her cheeks. Had Peng been right that the captain's hearing loss was a ruse?

Chapter 6

Will had smelled the sweet floral perfume of her skin the moment she entered his chamber. A different scent than the woman who had tended him earlier and brought him food he could not eat. She carried the odor of fish and wood smoke.

This one wasn't here to tend his wounds. The doctor had already poked and prodded him. But when the strange little man pulled out nine long, thin needles—four gold and five silver— Will waved him off, pushing them away. He had no idea what he wanted to do with them, but it couldn't have helped the gash on his head to be turned into a pincushion. Will pointed to his wound until the needle-wielding idiot understood. He stitched his head and gave him some bitter concoction to drink that made the room spin and darkened the edges of his vision.

What the hell did this one want? As he lay feigning sleep, wondering at her mission, she touched his hair.

It took him a moment to recognize her. Could it truly be Jian Jun who stood before him? Without her armor, matching scimitars, and commanding headdress, without the dark smear of kohl around her eyes, she looked so different. Softer. The hardness of her had lost its edge. Long shining hair shimmering almost blue black in the light as it reached past her waist. A thin robe of light silk wrapped tight around the slight curves of her body that was obviously naked beneath, if the proud peaks of her nipples were any indication. She looked like a totally different woman standing here. The only question was why?

She was speaking, or at least her mouth was working and her hands occasionally would emphasize some point. He wished he knew what she was professing in such an emphatic way.

It wasn't until he stood to wrap the sheet around him—the only choice to cover his own nakedness—did she miss a step and flinched. Her cheeks paled one moment only to flush a deep pink the next. He eyed her closely. Was she all right?

Will frowned. The movement tugged at the stitches holding his aching head together. His brain was still fuzzy from whatever the doctor gave him to drink. He had fallen into a deep sleep, but for how long? Hours could have passed. Time and day had been lost somewhere along the way. Time, day, his clothing, all his possessions, wealth, his ship, his crew, Tupper...

Perhaps that was why she was here. To bring him news of the others. To tell him Tupper had been found alive. Griffin, Hills, the rest of the men. Were they recovering nearby?

Will spied a quill and ink on a nearby table. He used it to scribble out, *My crew—have you had any news of how many have been rescued?*

He lifted the note for her to see, but at the look upon her face, he knew the answer before she shook her head. His mind screamed. Pain, anger and sorrow collided. This couldn't be. He couldn't be the sole survivor, could he?

Beneath his words, Jian Jun penned, *My men still search, but I am sorry none have been found. The storm was fierce, and the currents are strong and deep beyond The Brothers. I have little hope of finding their bodies, let alone anyone still alive at this point. You are lucky to have made it to shore.*

Lucky? A wave of grief flooded over him and nearly brought him to his knees. It was as if the air had been sucked from the room. He began to pace the small space like some caged beast with no hope of escape. *Lucky!* Aye, he was alive, but alone with nothing. No one. Was it lucky that he once again had to witness the sea claiming someone he loved? He could still see Tupper in that flash of lightning, shaking her fist at the heavens.

Pain punched Will in the chest. Jian Jun was staring at him with a horrible pitying look upon her lovely face. He couldn't even explain to her what he was feeling. His whole life, he'd lived in a world of silent isolation, but at least he'd had Tupper and a few others who cared enough to learn how to communicate with him.

Now there was no one.

Will covered his eyes with a hand. He'd lost bloody everything.... everything except his own miserable life. What kind of vicious cruelty was this?

The enormity of it all fell heavily upon him. His legs began to give way. Jian Jun was immediately at his side as his weight brought them both crashing down to the edge of the bed. He'd almost forgotten she was there. She shot to her feet as if the thin mattress were made of flames and picked up a brown glass vial from the nightstand. Jun placed a few drops in a cup of tea and held it to his lips. Her eyes urging him to drink. She tipped the delicate cup enough to give him a small sip. It was the same bitter concoction the doctor had given him to make him sleep. Ah…sleep. Deep and dreamless where he didn't have to remember. Didn't feel the pain of it all. If only he could sleep forever.

Without a second thought, Will snatched the brown glass from the table and drank the entire contents in one swift swallow. Jun's face registered her shock. He didn't care. If there were any justice in this world, the sour elixir would send him to a dark oblivion he would never wake from.

Will tossed the bottle aside and lay back upon the bed, rolling to his side. Blocking her and the rest of the world from his view. Waiting for the potion to take him away from his grief. He prayed the end would be swift.

* * * *

Jun watched in horror as the empty bottle skidded across the floor to land against the far wall. "You stupid fool, what have you done?"

Captain Quinn slumped back and rolled away from her. She then saw the two marks upon his back. Just as Yeh Tien-shih had reported. Faded red scars where someone had tried to kill this man in the past. And now, he was trying to finish the job himself?

An icy resolve slipped over her skin. "No, you don't."

She grabbed for the pot of cold tea and pulled against his shoulder to get him to roll over on his back. He frowned at her and tried to push her away, but she sat on his arm and held him as still as she could.

"Drink." She pushed the spout of the pot between his lips, but he stubbornly refused to open his mouth. "Damn it, open." Her angry gaze locked with his. "Do not fight me. I swear I will break your teeth!" She had to dilute that tincture, or get him to expel what he had taken and fast.

With her free hand she pinched shut his nose. When he opened his mouth to breathe, she poured. Beneath her, he sputtered and choked and tried to throw her off him, but she kept bucketing tea down his throat. He thrashed beneath her, but she covered his body with her own. Tea soaked them both, and the bed, but she kept forcing him to drink until he gave her a great shove off him and rushed to retch in the potted bamboo near the door.

Jun let out a grateful sigh, trying to calm her racing breath and pounding heart. The poor bamboo may be done for, but the captain wouldn't be dying, not tonight, anyway. It was then she realized she held his sheet. The man was dreadfully sick—and completely…breathtakingly naked.

She shook the distracting longing from her mind. Jun needed to get him back to bed and questioned her ability to do that on her own. But who would she summon to help her? Ting? Peng? No, she twisted her hair back out of the way and moved to his side. Jun's fingertips hovered over the puckered skin of his pistol scars before wrapping an arm around the captain's waist and doing her best to move him.

A good bit of sleeping potion would still have entered his bloodstream. If she didn't get him moving soon, he'd be dead weight and there would be no choice but to fetch help...and have to explain how she came to be alone with a naked man.

She tugged at him. "Come now. Please. Back to bed."

He turned, still on his knees, and hung tight to her leg, resting his head on her thigh. Jun slipped her free arm under his and attempted to lift him. To her relief, he started to rise. She braced herself as he used her body to pull himself to his feet. As he climbed her like a tree, the wrap of her robe shifted and twisted. In an odd dance, Jun got under his arm and was able to hold this hulking man upright.

By the time she wrestled them back to his bed, they were both struggling for breath. One shoulder of her robe hung loose to her elbow exposing half her chest, but it was his nakedness that most unnerved her. Had the scene not been so desperate and bizarre, she would have taken the time to appreciate the handsome view. The warmth of his body against hers. Skin against skin. *Oh, please.* Given his drugged state, the majesty of his body was not foremost in her mind. Jun bit her lip at the lie. *Damn it...concentrate!*

She tried to ease him back, but he slipped from her inadequate grasp and landed with a dull thud. Jun moved to rise and cover him, but in the shuffle, the tail of her robe had managed to get caught beneath his hip.

She raised pleading eyes to the heavens and begged for guidance. "Oh, Buddha, help me."

Before she could extricate herself, he touched her arm. Jun's gaze flew to his. His eyes were half closed, but he moved his hand to make a small gesture, touching his chin. She had no idea what it meant, but he repeated the motion. Was he asking for something?

Jun's heart still pounded in her ears as she tried to make sense of him. He reached out to her again. This time, he brushed the tangle of hair from her cheek right before his eyes closed and his hand fell to rest upon the curve of her bare breast.

She held her breath in the shock of surprise at his warm wide hand cradling her so intimately. He couldn't think after all this she wanted to have sex with him. Could he? The more alarming question was, did she?

Jun looked down and groaned. Half of her robe had been pulled away from her body revealing more than a single breast. Only the obi still held the garment to her waist. Why wouldn't he think she was offering herself to him? The only thing more damning would be if she were straddling the man.

Then, he snored.

Relief and indignation raged through her. Jun shoved his hand away, stood and yanked the silk of her robe out from beneath him, and finally threw the sheet over the rest of Captain Quinn.

Standing next to the bed, Jun jerked her clothing back into place and pushed the hair out of her eyes before dropping her face into her hands.

What foolishness had prompted her to come here? Thank goodness, none had seen her disgrace herself in such a way. However, past the shame of it all, a shimmer of pure desire trembled through her. She could still feel the heat of his body pressed against hers, his heavy touch upon her breast.

Lowering her hands, Jun gazed back at the sleeping captain. When was the last time a man had been so close to her or touched her so? She knew the answer to that. A slice of guilt passed through her, but she brushed it aside. It wasn't as if she had come in here ready to seduce the man, no matter how attractive she found him. Of course, now, she'd never be able to get the image of his sculpted body out of her mind. The rich smoothness of his skin…and the feel of his warm hand…

Jun tugged on her robe tightening it, straightening her shoulders and regaining her sanity. No good could come of such ridiculous thoughts. She'd been happily celibate since Jian Fu had died. Well, perhaps "happily" was not the correct word. What did it matter? She was far too busy ruling the empire he left under her command to concern herself with such frivolous things.

Her gaze once more ran the strong length of the captain. He really was beautiful. Now that she knew what lay beneath his sheet, of course she wanted him. She was not made of stone. Yes, she was hardened by the circumstance of her life, but beneath all the leather, steel, and weaponry, beyond being a pirate queen, she was still a living, breathing woman. A woman with needs and sexual desires.

And Captain Will Quinn was, without question, a most desirable man.

Chapter 7

Jun held her breath as Ting finished buckling the final straps of the tight breastplate to the rest of her armor. The cool steel made her nipples contract into hardened peaks. Ironic that a wide, rough, warm hand would have the same effect on her last night.

She couldn't get the scene out of her head. Couldn't get *him* out of her head. How awkward was it going to be seeing him? Exhaustion clouded her mind. It had only been a few hours since she had left his room, fearing if she stayed any longer she would surely be discovered. But she didn't dare leave before then.

The man had ingested enough sleeping potion to bring down a large ox. Even though she was successful in making him purge most of it, she had no way of knowing if he would stop breathing in the night without staying by his side.

It had meant a cold night on a hard floor, but when she left before dawn, his breathing still came deep and steady. The good captain's foolish attempt to end his life had failed. Thank goodness. However, the level of undress and the rush of sensation at his touch had only served to make her own breathing erratic at best.

Jun couldn't get the sight of him out of her mind. The more she tried, the worse it had become. Through those early hours as she sat on the hardness of that chilled floor, she had begun to imagine the scene ending in a much different way. As if Captain Quinn had not been drugged into unconsciousness. As if his intimate touch had not been an accident...

Perhaps he would have kneaded the sensitive flesh of her breast and teased the firming peak of her nipple, rolling it gently between his wide fingers before leaning forward and taking it into his mouth. His eager hands pushing down the rest of her robe, spreading its hems, spreading her legs.

Impatience driving his heated touch up the inside of her thigh…

"Mistress, are you unwell?"

Ting's concerned looked jerked Jun back into the present.

Jun stepped back, and turned away. Heat rushed to her cheeks and other susceptible areas. She gasped a breath. "I'm perfectly fine."

"You're trembling and flushed. Shall I fetch the physician?"

It was not a doctor she needed. The sight of the captain's naked body flashed in her mind's eye again. Jun nearly moaned at the rush of desire that settled hot and damp between her thighs. Had it not taken more than twenty minutes to don her heavy armor, she would have torn it from her body and jumped naked into one of her koi ponds to extinguish the building heat.

She turned back to Ting, notched her chin and composed herself. "The morning is already warm and steamy, promising a sultry day, that is all. Help me secure my hair."

Ting eyed her warily. "Of course, Mistress."

Hair… Her mind returned to the heavy ropes of his thick woolen hair, that had been surprisingly heavy and soft, and the rasp of beard that darkened his jaw had accentuated the shape of his mouth. Beautiful full lips. What would his kisses be like? Jun brushed her fingertips over her mouth.

She did moan then—aloud—startling Ting once more. Jun cleared her throat and moved to gather her weapons. "Were you able to get proper clothing for our guest?"

Ting handed Jun the final addition to her uniform, the unwieldy headdress that sat so heavy some days it pained her head. "Aye, the tailor spent a sleepless night, but delivered the garments you requested at first light."

The tailor wasn't the only one. It would be a long day, as well. Longer still if she couldn't control her lurid musings. "Any other word this morning."

"A flurry in the great hall. Several items found on the north beach have been gathered at the shore. They await your inspection. Perhaps from the stranger's…pardon, Captain Quinn's ship?"

Hope bloomed in her chest. "Any more survivors? Bodies?"

"No, mistress."

Through her long night, beyond her ridiculous fantasies, Jun wished to have better news for him come first light, but it seemed the storm had spared just one member of the *Scarlet Night*. Living with such guilt would be a lifetime's burden for him. After his desperate reaction last night, she worried if he would ever recover from such a tragedy.

"When you delivered the Captain's clothing, was he awake?" Jun did her best to appear nonchalant when concern still nibbled at her.

"Aye, mistress." Ting nodded.

Relief raised Jun's spirits. She would keep him close. For protective reasons, of course. She was...concerned. This way she could keep him under strict scrutiny over the next few days without revealing her reasons why. After all, how would she explain her late night visit, and more so, to protect Captain Quinn from losing face. He'd already lost enough. "Please bring him to the hall."

"As you wish."

* * * *

All stood when Jun entered and gave her the proper bow of respect. Just once, she would like to slip unnoticed into a room and see something other than the tops of heads, but it was the price she paid. At the clap of her hands, everyone returned to their duties.

Jun took her place on the dais. Next to her seat of power, was a table laden with the day's business and a pot of steaming tea. An eager servant stood at the ready. A bead of sweat had already started to trickle down the channel of her spine. Hot tea was not what she wanted. Jun waved the girl away. What she desired most was...

Captain Quinn entered from the east like a shadowed sun. Following Ting, he moved with the grace of a sinuous cat. He stood tall. Head up. His gaze scanning the room as if searching for a familiar face in the crowd.

The addition of a proper cotton changshan with the wide-legged pants and long wrapped tunic did nothing to blend him into the crowd around him. Quite the opposite. The tailor must have misjudged the breadth of Captain Quinn's chest as the wrapping was not as overlapped and reserved as it should be.

Jun raised an eyebrow and imagined Genghis Khan himself would not have made such an impressive figure upon entering a room. The captain was built like a mountain, yet he moved like a warrior, all sinew and barely disguised danger. She needed to learn more about the *Scarlet Night*. Captain Quinn did not appear to be like any merchant she had ever seen.

As he approached, Jun stood and waited until his gaze landed on her. She tried to read his face. Decipher his thoughts. Did he recall the events of last night? His glance registered no signs of it until he made a slow, deliberate sweep of her body from top to bottom and back again, resting briefly a few inches below her throat before lifting his heated gaze back to hers. Jun's skin fairly sizzled.

Oh, yes, he remembered.

Jun's face burned as the trickle of moisture reached the base of her spine. He missed nothing with those all-seeing eyes of his. And yet, he gave nothing away. No frown, no smirk, no indication as to what he might be feeling or thinking.

"He looks the fool in those clothes." Peng startled Jun. She hadn't seen him enter the hall, nor had she paid any notice of him sidling up to her.

Jun returned her attention to her work before she burst into flames. "Would you rather him in rags?" *Or nothing at all...*

"I would rather him behind bars, but my advice is falling on deaf ears." He huffed. "How ironic."

Jun narrowed her eyes at Peng. There was a deep protective bone in her body. Reserved for few in her life, but fierce nonetheless. After last night, her sense of that protectiveness toward the captain was one more thing forged within her. "Humor is not your gift, Chou Peng."

She turned her back on him and retrieved a long-handled bag made of thick woven cotton containing two items she'd requested last evening—a small square of stone tile, and a bit of gypsum. Tools for the captain a bit more transportable than ink and quill. Qi had given Jun the idea for the gift. The child loved to draw pictures on the stones in the gardens and would then dance upon them to scuff her bare feet over the scribbles to erase them and start anew.

Jun slipped the long strap over her shoulder and pulled the stone from the bag. To Peng, she asked, "It is my understanding your men have gathered a cache of recovered items on the north beach. Is that correct?"

"It is." Peng eyed the stone in her hands with curiosity.

"No human remains? Signs of anyone else coming ashore?"

"None."

Jun frowned. "It is doubtful anyone could have fought their way to our brother island Salahnama?"

"The shoreline is much too steep. They could have fought the currents, but it is likely they would not have been able to climb the sheer walls." Peng tipped his sharp chin in Captain Quinn's direction before smoothing his beard back into a well-groomed point. "If his fellow crewmates did not make their way here in the hour following the storm, I'm afraid there is little hope for them at this point."

"I agree."

During the exchange, Jun noted the way the captain's attention never wavered from them. He studied them intently, watching their mouths, following every movement of their hands. Her understanding of what life might be like for him grew, as did her curiosity to learn how he had overcome what to her seemed an impossible challenge. If it were true that he was the Captain of the *Scarlet Night*, how had he commanded? How had he survived the rugged conditions aboard ship without being able to hear and speak? Lived a life at sea? How had that all come to be? Either he was an accomplished liar, or he was a most remarkable man.

When his perceptive pale eyes captured hers, they caused her breath to hitch. No...he wasn't lying.

"Good morning, Captain." As she spoke, she used the soft gypsum to write the words on the flat stone pad. Using her palm, she rubbed the words away and wrote more. *You will please come with us to the north beach.* Jun held up the stone for him to read. He gave the tiniest frown. She repeated the erasing and continued. *We believe items from your ship have been recovered.*

He held out his hands and reached for the stone before using the back of his wide palm to wipe her words away. The captain scribbled one word and held the slate for her to see. *Anyone?*

Jun's heart still broke for him. He continued to hold out hope that others from his crew had survived. It pained her to have to continue to dash his hopes. She gave him the smallest shake of her head before placing a comforting hand on his arm. The muscle in his jaw pulsed as he wiped away the word and handed her back the tile.

"Are we done with the pleasantries?" Peng hissed. His arms folded tight within his sleeves across his chest. "My men are waiting." He spoke to her in Chinese, for all to hear.

Jun met Peng's glare with one of her own. "And they shall wait as long as I demand they wait."

"As you wish." He bit out the words.

Jun was not a patient woman. Nor a tolerant one. And no one knew that more than Peng, and yet there he stood almost taunting her with his insolence. Perhaps she had given him too many liberties and made him boldly think he could exceed his station. She would respect him, however, and not reprimand him and cause him to lose face in front of his men, but this was far from over.

"Mind yourself," she added in English with a false calm to her voice before stepping off the dais and leading the way.

Captain Quinn fell into step at her side. Peng rushed to catch up with her. "It isn't necessary for you to accompany us, my men and I can see to this insignificant duty."

Jun didn't look at him. "I'm coming."

"To see a pile of rubble and waterlogged chests?" Peng's disdain laced his words.

Jun never broke stride, but pulled one razor-sharp scimitar from its tooled sheath. "I'm coming, and that is my final word."

Chapter 8

All Will's senses were on high alert even though part of his brain was still a bit muddled this morning. The humid air did little to clear his thoughts. He clipped his pace to stay alongside Jian Jun. As she swung her arm the flash off the tip of her sword kept pace with each determined stride. They passed through the halls and out into the haze of the day. On the way, each person stopped in their chores to honor Jun's arrival. With or without her blade, she commanded these people. Her power was undeniable and impressive. Out of respect, he let her take the lead, cut his gait once more to match that of her sneering purple companion. She led them toward the harbor.

Will had no clue what words she and the other man had shared, but the tension between the pair was high. His distrust toward Will needed no interpretation, but there was something more Will couldn't put his finger on. Something had transpired. While Jun and Will passed their communication slate back and forth, the man's expression had darkened, but Will had missed it happening.

But the man's fists were balled at his sides and he moved as if he had a ship's mast jammed up his arse. A lover's quarrel perhaps? Whatever the cause of his mood, back in the great hall, Jun had held all Will's attention for a moment too long, and he'd lost the opportunity to read the man properly.

She'd distracted him. Will wasn't usually so distracted. Being unfocused was a danger he couldn't afford, but in her presence his feet felt as if he were standing on shifting sands.

Last night's events had rushed back into his consciousness upon seeing her. He was struck by the difference between the hardened pirate leader upon the dais, and the woman who appeared in his room. Internally, he groaned. *And what did I do? Tried to do myself in. I'm a bloody idiot!*

Will struggled for some valid excuse to explain his reckless, cowardly behavior. He'd been out of his mind. Grief and pain had temporarily won the battle. The lure of an endless sleep had been so seductive. Was there any other justification for what he had tried to do?

But there she'd been, looking soft and beautiful. Not a hard edge in sight. She'd saved his sorry arse, too, practically drowning him in tea. After that, his memory was a bit sketchy. The pull of the drugs had dragged him into a dangerous spiral. Next thing he knew he was face first in a plant hurling up the sour contents of his stomach and half his toenails. How he got back to bed, he couldn't guess. He'd been naked, that was for sure. Had he been stupid enough to try and seduce her? The only thing he recalled with any amount of clarity was the sight of her perfectly naked breast. Small and creamy white. Her nipple, the palest shade of palest pink. All he'd wanted in that hazy moment was to taste her. Begin with her lips before moving his mouth lower to sip on the delicately blushed tip. He'd reached for her to pull her mouth to his. And then it was morning, and he was alone.

Watching the straight line of her back as she walked along the docks, Will held on to that lusty vision of that one perfect breast. He was actually thankful for the distraction. It may be the only thing keeping him sane today.

Will took in the sights around him. The streets and docks bustled with the village's morning activity. Ships being loaded and unloaded. Merchants, seamen, and peddlers already busy with the day's business. The harbor was full of every manner and size of ship. Mostly junks. Some as long as the largest frigate. Their odd sails with their long bamboo slats opened and closed like giant ladies' fans were folded closed at anchor. High sterns, projected square bows. Some carried as many as five masts. Those he could see all flew the flag of Jian Jun's fleet with its golden dragon breathing fire on a field of black. Red flags of luck decorated each mast. Their rich color reminded him of the *Scarlet Night*.

The responsibility for the wreck still hung heavy on this heart, and walking past the impressive line of ships filling the docks, he braced himself for another blinding wave of grief at seeing what remained of his own beautiful ship.

Ahead of him he spied the familiar red of her sails in a sodden heap at the water's edge. Jian Jun and her officer stopped, yet a flood of emotion propelled Will past them. Rope and sail and a shattered section of polished railing told him the final chapter of the tale. He lifted a sliver of wood, crushing it in his fist until the sharp edge cut into his palm. Will curled into the ache in his chest. This heap…rubble… How could this be the last scene of his great ship and all who sailed upon her? He searched the waters but all he could see was the haunting sight of her angled masts against the storm.

The power of the seas had been too great. They hadn't had a chance. The *Night* had broken up at the incessant battering of the sea's fists as it floundered against the reef. She'd been reduced to bits.

Will looked back over the items dumped on the sand. He used his toe to ease the shredded sail aside. Several trunks, a belay pin, part of a barrel, and several lengths of deck board were all that remained. He pulled the trunks free from the rest.

Crossing to one of Jun's men, he pointed to the heavy dirk the man carried at his side. Will held his hand out for the weapon and stared the man down before watching his brief questioning glance toward his commander. At Jun's slight nod, the man pulled the dagger from its sheath and handed it over, handle first.

Flipping the weapon in his hand, Will used the solid hilt to break open the locks on each trunk. His stomach dropped when he raised their lids and found everything inside ruined. An entire bow-topped chest full of bolts of rich silks had been reduced to a casket of dripping, useless rags. He hauled fists full out to puddle on the sand. Will opened the next. A cache of expensive spices now resembled rusted mud. He scooped the muck with his fingers before throwing it aside in disgust.

Will straightened and kicked over each trunk in frustration. He searched the rest of the wreckage. This was it? The truth gnawed at his belly. Chests of gold and silver rarely floated, and anything that did was ruined. He'd truly lost everything...and everyone.

There was one thing he wanted from this mess. Needed. Moving to the yards of heavy wet sail, Will used the dirk he'd borrowed to cut away several ragged pieces of the once majestic, ruby-dyed sail canvas that proudly bowed from each mast of the *Scarlet Night.* It was the ship's signature. It's identity. Their calling card to their enemies that the mighty crew of the *Night* were upon them. A magnificent sight as well as a chilling one.

Her red sails had always called him home. He'd grown up in her rigging. Known every inch of board, every nail, and every gun. He'd fought on her decks with his back anchored firmly to her center mast and believed as a boy, when he stood in the crow's nest and held his arms wide, that he was truly flying. A tightening in his throat threatened to choke him. Now look at her. She was a pile of sea trash.

Will took the smaller square of red sail and tucked it into the front of his tunic where it lay cold and wet against his heart. The second, larger piece, he had other plans for. As captain, he had one final duty to perform for his crew.

He nudged at the pile again with a bare toe as he swallowed past the lump in his gullet. How could things have ended so quickly and completely? Was this truly all that remained? Shouldn't there be more of such a magnificent ship and her brave crew?

A glint of brass caught the light of the sultry sun. Will tipped his head and peered past the tangle of rope. *Bloody hell.* Hope surged in him as he pushed back the remainder of the sails and shredded rigging and pulled his log box from the wreckage.

Crouching before the small chest, he ran his hand over the rich carving. Packed sand filled the pattern. Could the ship's logs have survived? After opening the other chests and finding everything ruined, he didn't dare raise his expectations. Using the point of the dirk's blade, he inserted the tip into the iron lock. After a moment of finessing the hasp, he felt the distinctive pop as the lid released.

They were lost, they had to be. Will sat back on his heels and waited a full breath, closing his eyes before daring to lift the lid.

When he looked, there they were—his precious logbooks. Damp and curled at the edges, their leather covers stained with salty halos of seawater, but the chest had done its best holding the pounding waves at bay. Given what little was left of the ship, it was nothing short of a miracle to be holding the logs in his hands.

Will gathered the small chest along with the scrap of *Scarlet's* sail and rose to his feet. He pulled a deep breath into his sore lungs as he scanned the white beach. Would he ever stop looking for them? After all this time, it was foolish to hope. Still he gave a final look expecting to find another member of his crew. Some evidence at least. Alive or dead. However, the wide sands were clear.

Faces of forty-two men…and one extraordinary woman…flashed through his mind. He feared their final moments, their ultimate fates would haunt him all his days. Will rubbed a hand over his eyes. The tension in his jaw threatened to crush his back teeth. Thirty years of faces paraded through his thoughts. The *Scarlet Night* had been their legacy as well. He'd remember them all. Ric, MacTavish, Neo…Gavin… They'd entrusted him to carry on after they left.

He'd failed them.

When he took command, he believed somehow that Gavin would have been proud. Will failed him as well. He and Tupper had given him a life. It wasn't right that he was standing here, the heat of the sun warm on his skin. The clean cool air coming from the sea filling his nostrils. Why should he be the one standing on this shore? He should have gone down with the rest. After all he was Captain. A captain goes down with their ship. If anyone should be dead, it was him. It was his fault they were lost. In his blind rush to save one, he had killed them all.

Will tucked the last treasure of his command under his arm and turned back toward the palace. As he passed Jun's man, Will returned his dagger and kept walking.

Where Jun and her purple shadow stopped, two servants stood on either side of them, holding poles stretching heavy cloth over their heads to provide shade against the brutal sun. When he reached them, Jun moved to join him, and the servants scrambled to follow until she waved them away. Once more, Will was reminded of her station. Her rank among her people. She truly was their queen.

Then he saw them. Heads. Twenty or so severed heads on pikes lined the entrance to the harbor. What had these men done, and how had he missed them before? Were they enemies? They had obviously been placed here to send a clear, brutal message.

Jun paid them no mind, and simply walked past taking the lead once more. Her companion, however, made a point to lift his gaze to the gruesome sight and cast a smug glance in Will's direction. He lifted one eyebrow and tipped the blade of his chin toward him. Was he giving Will a warning? Reminding him of exactly how ruthless their queen could be?

The man forgot one thing. Will was no babe in short pants. Hell, he'd never been a babe in short pants. He'd lay good coin on the fact that he'd lived as a pirate longer than either of them. Heads on pikes neither shocked nor frightened him. Neither did purple-draped idiots that dared challenge him.

Will shot a glance at Jun's proud back once again. He shifted the chest under his arm. One thing was certain. The longer he stayed here, the more tenuous the situation. Jian Jun had been gracious so far, but he'd seen enough to be wary of such generosity. They were pirates after all. Fierce. Greedy. Rarely did they act out of the goodness of their hearts without some selfish motive.

He'd need a few things before leaving, however. A weapon, surely. Truth be told he felt naked without a single blade. How he'd come by one, he hadn't figured out. You didn't just ask for a pistol, and stealing one might put his own head on a pike.

Will winced as his foot met with an arch-stabbing stone. He ground his back teeth at the sharp pain. And bloody boots. He couldn't run around barefoot any more. The strange clothing, he could deal with even if it fit him poorly, but he needed proper footwear. His mind flashed to the memory of his favorite boots filling with seawater and being dragged away from him during his battle with the storm. He'd just gotten the damn things broken in. Looking at those around him, the men all had such small feet by comparison. There must be someone with feet his size, but without funds, how would he acquire a pair even if he could find them?

So he'd need a decent weapon...preferably two or three, and a sturdy pair of boots. He ticked them off in his mind. And there was that other thing every good pirate captain required. Beyond a mighty crew and fair seas.

Will looked out in to the harbor pack tight with craft, scanning once more the odd junks resting at anchor. The last thing on the list would require all his honed skills and a few he hadn't learned yet. Because somehow, some way, either by beg, borrow, or steal, he needed a bloody new ship.

Chapter 9

"And what do you propose we do with him now?" Peng spoke over her right shoulder as they proceeded back to the palace.

"I haven't decided." Jun kept moving. Ahead of her walked Captain Quinn. His long strides distancing him from her. Her bumbling servants in charge of shading them from the sun's heat scrambled to keep up. The warmth of the day was only half of the slow heat building within her. Oh yes, she had some distinct ideas as to what she'd like to do with the good Captain. None of which she was willing to share with Chou Peng.

"May I make a humble suggestion?"

Jun's jaw tightened. With Peng, nothing was ever humble and Jun was certain she knew what his suggestion might be. "When have I ever prevented you from speaking your mind?"

"It is a small boon for us that he's retrieved what appears to be his ship's logs. I say we confiscate them at once. They would hold all the information we would want regarding his journey here. He appears well enough to be put into service. Certainly, he cannot be used upon one of our ships, but as a slave…"

Jun stopped and turned back to Peng. "Why wouldn't he be able to join one of our crews?"

Peng waved a hand in Captain Quinn's direction. "The man cannot hear for one thing. He's hardly fit for a life of pirating."

"Have you forgotten that he captained his own ship?"

"So he scribbled on a bit of parchment." Peng continued to point at the captain's back. "How do we know he isn't lying to us? I've never heard of a deaf seaman before, let alone a deaf captain. Was he sailing a merchant ship? How would he have led a crew? He doesn't even speak. How would he have issued a simple order? Did this alleged crew read his mind?" He indicated the bag she still carried. "Write each other notes on stones? We don't even know if he truly is who he says he is."

The urge to vehemently defend Will caught Jun by surprise. Her jaw tightened again. Sweat slid down from her headdress to dampen her temple.

Peng continued. "You assume a great many things about this man, and I'm curious as to why. You're not usually one to overlook such vital facts. Take those books from him. I bet they will confirm my suspicions if nothing else. Let me and my men interrogate him fully. If he's lying, I'll get the truth out of him one way or another. And then I say put him in chains. He has a strong back. We can use it maintaining our fleet, scraping hulls, mending nets. Make him pay for our hospitality."

"And what if you're wrong?" She tipped her head at Peng.

He gave her a smug smile while tugging at his beard. "I'm not."

Jun turned away. "I think you are." She kept walking.

"Your reaction to this man is most disturbing. I've never known you to be so blinded." Peng's accusing tone rankled her. "What hold does he have upon you?"

A very tender hold. In Jun's mind, a gentle hand cradled her overheated breast. She closed her eyes to another heated rush.

Shaking the image from her thoughts she turned back to Peng in exasperation. "You think stripping this man of the one possession he still claims and making him a slave is the proper thing to do?"

"How else will we get our hands on those logs?"

"I don't suppose we could…" Jun spread her arms wide. "Oh, let me just toss this insane idea about… Why don't we simply ask him to see them?"

"He'll not show us." Peng hissed.

Jun planting her hands on her hips. "He'll show them to me. In good time, I'll get him to hand them to me of his own will. You know, some things do not require brute force to obtain. Not everything needs to happen at the broad threat of your blade."

The muscle in his jaw pulsed. "I put my original question back to you, then. What are we to do with him?"

She glanced back at the "him" in question. "Whatever I deem appropriate." Jun caught Will appraising the ships in the harbor. "I'm not convinced he wouldn't make a fine addition to one of our crews. Or perhaps I will keep him here. He makes quite the imposing figure. Perhaps a private guard?"

"I don't think it's wise to keep him so close."

We couldn't get too much closer than we did last night. "Some of these decisions may not be ours."

"It would be if we stopped treating him as a distinguished guest and more of the intruder he is." Peng's voice rose.

It was obvious their disagreement would continue to circle upon itself. Jun tried to placate him. "Patience, I understand your concern, but I'd like to take some time to learn all I can about Captain Quinn and his travels here. Information is power. If I'm to gather that power, I need to get him to relax and confide in me. Trust me. I think it would, therefore, be wise to give him the freedom to come and go as he pleases."

Peng blew a frustrated breath and held her gaze for a long moment. "At least, allow me to send word through the fleet asking if anyone knows of a ship called the *Scarlet Night.* While we wait, let me put a watch on him should he leave the walls of the palace. He can't be allowed free run of the village. Not until we learn his full story."

"Fine, but keep your man at a fair distance. I don't want him to know he's being followed." The idea that Peng's man might make it difficult for her to spend time with Captain Quinn alone had her emphasizing one key point. "And only when he leaves the palace. Otherwise, I will personally see to the man and find out what I can."

"I still don't like the idea of you spending so much time with him."

Jun tipped her head and gave him a hard stare. "What is it you fear, Peng? Not my physical harm, surely. Do you worry about my reputation? Or perhaps you're concerned that he will seduce me? That the sight of a handsome man might turn my head? Turn me into a blushing schoolgirl? Make me forget who I am and jeopardize all I have worked so hard to achieve?"

"Possibly." Peng didn't even have the decency to look ashamed.

"You have forgotten one thing. I am the ice queen." She turned her back on him and strode away, following the broad back of Captain Quinn. His long stride emphasizing the shape of his legs and backside. *And I'll decide when and with whom I choose to thaw…*

* * * *

Back in the great hall, Jun lost sight of Captain Quinn as she was surrounded by her constant responsibilities. It was only later, after dismissing the scribes and ministers, that she could seek him out.

Blissfully, she'd shed her heavy headdress and armor for a cooler tunic, but remained in her black wardrobe. Her hair trailed in a single braid down the center of her back. Her excuse to find him was valid should anyone question, still the eyes of the hall watched as she moved toward the east corridor.

She carried a small bowl of fruit, having not seen him at the noon meal. The writing stone hung from one shoulder. At this hour of the day, she encountered several curious servants who startled at seeing her and scrambled to bow at her passing. Even given the proper purpose of her visit to the captain's rooms, she couldn't help but feel a flush of guilt. Had she not snuck down these same corridors last night...and been plagued by sultry thoughts all morning...

Standing before his door, Jun paused, uncertain. Unlike last night, she was not slipping into a sleeping man's room like the mist off the sea. Yet how does one knock on the door of a deaf man?

The air in the corridor was stale and stuffy. The air in his room was not any better when she entered. Her tunic clung to her skin. Will's back was to her, and she took a moment to once again admire the wide set of his shoulders as he toiled at a task. He was washing. Or at least he was working at his bowl and pitcher.

As she watched him, he stopped, straightened his back. Lifting his chin, he sniffed the air like an animal sensing a predator. Coiled like a taught spring, he spun around. His one hand reaching for a weapon that wasn't there. The other clutched a dripping scrap of red sail.

Jun held up one hand in surrender. "It's only me. I'm sorry, I startled you. Didn't mean to intrude."

Upon seeing her his shoulders lowered and he visibly relaxed. Giving her a small nod, he returned the sodden sail back into the bowl before drying his hands. The wide sleeves of his shirt were rolled back to his elbows revealing strong tanned forearms.

"I wasn't sure how to make my presence known to you before coming in." He watched her mouth. It made her self-conscious. She bit the inside of her lip. "I thought you might be hungry." Jun raised the bowl she carried.

He made a small gesture by quickly touching the tips of his fingers against his chin before taking the fruit from her hands. Wasn't that the same gesture he made last night? He set the bowl aside.

She started to tell him he should eat to rebuild his strength, but stopped and remembered with a start the bag she held. Jun raised it so he could see, and pulled the writing slate and gypsum.

I'm sorry I try to speak with you, when you cannot understand. Jun wrote the words and turned the slate for him to see before scrubbing the back of her hand over the slate and continuing. *I wanted you to have this.* She tapped the stone. *I apologize for disturbing you.*

The captain took the slate, erased what she wrote and simply scribbled. *Didn't.*

"Man of few words," Jun spoke to herself. The intensity of his stare made her uneasy. "You may not hear me, yet you miss nothing. As if you sense the words. Feel them."

He lifted his eyes from her mouth to pin her with his gaze. Tapping the slate, he handed it back to her. Jun was at a sudden loss for words herself. With so much to say and to ask, where should she begin? Glancing about the room, she noted the log box resting upon the floor next to the bed. She also realized the washing he was tending to when she entered was the piece of sail he had saved from the wreckage of his ship.

I am so very sorry for your loss, Captain Quinn, she wrote. *We never harden to the loss of our crewmates.*

He shook his head slowly.

How many were lost? Jun held up the slate.

With his long, wide fingers he indicated the number forty-three.

Terrible loss. Jun wrote.

He nodded, then sat on the edge of his bed. He motioned for her to sit with him. When she did he took the slate from her.

I thank you for what you did last night. He paused to give her time to read before continuing. *Not in my right mind.*

Jun met his gaze and placed a gentle hand on his arm in reply. She struggled for the words to ease his pain, make it better for him. Tell him she understood the kind of devastation he'd suffered. Before she could, he continued writing.

Appreciate your hospitality, Will move on as soon as I'm able.

Move on? No. She was quick to take the slate. *You're free to stay as long as you need, Captain.*

Call me Will.

Jun smiled. "Will." She repeated it. Twice. She liked the way it sounded. It was a good strong name. She nodded and said it again. A pure expression of wonder crossed over his face as he watched her mouth. She covered her lips with her fingertips. The room was already stifling, yet heat rose to her cheeks. Her clothing clung to her damp skin. Simple breathing became a race against the beating of her heart. His stare flustered her. When had simply saying a man's name become so intimate?

Averting her eyes from the power of his gaze, she wrote under his words, *You must call me Jun.*

Will made several gestures with his hands. He pointed to the slate and made an odd sweeping movement using his pinkie finger alongside his chin. Was that how he said her name? When she mimicked him with the same motion, he smiled. A stunning white smile. It was if the clouds parted and the sun blazed out from behind. The effect was intoxicating. The race was over. Jun's breath caught in her chest.

He then pointed to his own name and showed her how to hold three fingers wide before tapping his temple. All at once, Jun was an inquisitive child again learning new words at her mother's elbow. "Will," she signed as she said the word, then smiled back at him.

Will nodded with approval. It took all Jun's resolve not to throw her arms around his neck and kiss his beautiful, grinning lips.

Chapter 10

Watching Jun sign his name was like getting hit in the chest…with a cannonball. When had such a simple thing taken on such an extraordinary meaning? She looked so pleased with herself at learning the two simple signs of their names. She reminded him briefly of another.

Other than Tupper, there had only been one woman in his life that had bothered to learn how to communicate with him. The image of Samantha Christian flashed through his mind.

Samantha had come aboard the *Scarlet Night* dressed as a cabin boy to escape from Virginia several years ago. He'd lost his young heart to her, and quickly had it handed back to him on a bloody platter. The two holes in his back were a painful reminder that he had foolishly fallen in love with a woman who had fallen in love with someone else.

But Samantha had never known him as Will. She only called him Bump. And Tupper, too. Griffin and the crew referred to him only as Captain.

Jian Jun was the first then. That single realization launched another cannonball.

Bloody hell.

Her eyes sparkled with excitement. A pink blush brightened the tops of her cheeks. The warmth of the room had added a shimmer to her face, her throat, to the vee of pale skin leading into the top of her blouse toward the gentle valley between her breasts. He imagined finding a different warmth there.

Good God, man. She only signed your name.

Will stood before he did something to earn him two more holes in his back. He'd been rinsing the sand and salt out of the bit of *Scarlet*'s sail when she'd came in. He returned to the bowl and wrung out the bit of cloth. After it dried, he'd write the names of the forty-three on its cloth and attend to their souls.

Turning back to Jun, he was once again struck by her beauty. Even dressed in trousers and tall boots like a man, even knowing of her power and strength, she couldn't hide her womanly appeal. He'd already seen the soft edges of her. Will refused to admit he had somehow dreamed the vision of her delicate breasts. Looking at her now, through her clinging clothing, he could imagine the rest of her.

Thank goodness what his tunic lacked in width, it more than adequately made up in length. Still he tugged at its hem to hide the hardening evidence of his lustful musings. Had the water in that bowl not been full of sand and grit, he'd have gladly used it to douse the flames in his pants.

Jun wrote something else on the slate before holding it up to him. *There is no air in this room.* She plucked at her neckline.

He couldn't agree more.

She continued. *You should come visit my gardens. They are lovely and cool.*

Will hesitated, fixing her with a stare. Jun quickly scribbled, *We could share our evening meal there if you'd like?*

Said Eve as she offered the apple.

Will stifled a smirk at his thoughts. Spending an evening with her in a garden was tempting, but he needed to keep his head. This was Jian Jun after all. She was fond of removing heads from fools stupid enough to underestimate her. Was a blissful dinner all she was after? Caution would be wise. Regardless of his body's obvious want of her, his mind warned him against her. This is exactly how the two, his body and his head, would lose touch with one another. Had those twenty heads decorating the harbor been dinner dates as well?

Still, an evening enjoying a cool meal surrounded by her beauty might be worth losing his head. Perhaps he could coax her into giving him one of her many ships. Surely she wouldn't miss one small junk. *'I would be honored,'* he signed with a bow before stepping to retrieve the slate and answering, *Yes.*

Jun smiled her pleasure at his answer. She stood then and pressed her palm to her pinked cheeks. Looking about the room, she said something. Perhaps remarking on the heat once again, but then her attention was captured by the box at her feet. Jun bent to retrieve it, running her fingertips over the ornate carving on its lid after she rested it on the bed.

Will's earlier caution flared. Did she know he was a pirate? Would she see him as a threat to her and her fleet? Or the price on his head would make her a tidy profit for turning his arse over to the British. Certainly, all the evidence she would need to hang him was in that box. Accounts of conquests, tallies of bounty, the names of the ships they'd attacked. The

Scarlet Night was not as well known in this sector of the world, so she could just as easily believe him to be a wayward merchant. It might be safer for him if she did.

He was quick to ease it out of her grasp. The last thing he wanted was to heighten her curiosity, but these were secrets he would be wise to keep. Will moved the box back to the floor and did the only thing he could think of to disguise his action. Taking her hand, he placed it over his heart and covered it with his own.

Surprised eyes met his as he then lifted her hand and turned it over to press his lips to her palm. He sensed the slight tremor radiate through her and smiled. Oh, yes, she wasn't thinking about his logs anymore.

Several hours later, he headed toward Jian Jun's secluded quarters. Her maid, Ting, led him through the great hall. Long shafts of late afternoon light sliced through the haze and highlighted the intricate patterns in the floor's inlay. Jun's first mate, General Chou Peng, glared at Will as he passed. He'd asked Jun his name earlier. She'd laughed when he referred to him as the skinny sea urchin in royal king's robes. The description fit him perfectly, however.

Jun indicated that Peng had been with her as her first mate for years, and she relied on him a good deal. Will decided it would be wise to give the man a wide berth. If he were to get off this island, he'd have to mind where he stepped. Chou Peng may not look like a physical threat, but might and brawn were not necessary when the man had Jun's entire fleet at his disposal.

Ting touched his sleeve to get his attention. A gentle woman with a scrubbed, wide face, and hair pulled taut into a thin braid that reached clear to the back of her knees. He learned her name as well when Jun informed him, Ting would come gather him for their dinner. She pointed to a narrow door set behind the dais where Jun sat to oversee her empire. Standing to one side she bowed low as he passed. Her braid slipped over her shoulder.

Will entered Jun's private oasis. Exotic smells of flowers and moist, cool earth filled the space. The room itself was nothing like he expected. It was as if he had stepped out of the great hall into another world. A feminine oasis. Muted shades of color adorned the modest furnishings, tall vases spilled an overflow of flowers, and plants of all description set in decorative pots crowded every corner. Door frames, rounded on the tops, continued the shape of the domed ceiling painted with a pale sky and pink tinged clouds. Sheer curtains danced in the breeze coming from twin sets of doors that stood open leading out into a magnificent outer courtyard.

Vines draped and curtained the doorway, beckoning him to enter. Crushed shelled pathways led the way to curve and swirl among the plantings. Tropical flowers he couldn't begin to identify cast their sweet scent into the air. Lanterns had already been lit to combat the approaching darkness. Their light caught in a series of round pools and tumbling water. Its source hidden by smooth barked palms. A natural stream perhaps?

Jun sat looking impossibly beautiful strumming a lute of some sort. Her eyes closed, she held the instrument upright in her lap. The long shining curtain of her hair concealing a portion of her face as she plucked at the strings.

There were few times in Will's life that he'd wished he was anything more than he was, but if he could hear the world for a single moment… He stood in the growing shadows and longed for that moment to be now.

Jun opened her eyes and grinned before putting the instrument to one side and standing. She wore a silk gown in pinks and golds. Embroidered birds in silver and gold thread captured the light. Will couldn't remember a time when he had seen anything so lovely.

As much as Jun dominated the harsh and brutal world beyond these cloistered walls, she embodied the exquisite beauty of these gardens as well. How could one woman have such diametrically opposite sides? Will admired and respected Jun's role of pirate empress. The sheer number of her fleet rivaled many countries.

And yet, the other facet—the gentle refined elegance of her caught him so completely by surprise, it took him a moment to process it. It was as if there were two distinct women separated by a single, narrow door.

Dark eyes held his. Fingers of seduction wrapped around him. He could picture her stripped of the last bit of the world beyond this haven and pulling her naked body to his. Laying her amongst the plants. Forgetting anything else existed, save them.

Jun was speaking. Walking toward him. A wave of pure lust threatened to capsize him. When she placed a delicate hand on his arm, he could do nothing but stare at the gentle taper of her fingers.

Then she swept a hand indicating a small, low table, which had been tucked into one of the garden's fern-created alcoves. Two fat cushions flanked the table full of an abundance of various foods. Bright fruits piled high alongside bowls of pink shrimp. Roasted meats mixed with an array of vegetables sat in rings of rice and noodles. It was a feast.

Jun motioned for him to sit. Will folded his long legs and lowered himself on to one of the cushions. She pulled the second pillowed tuft close and kneeled herself. All the while her mouth moved as she spoke silent words to him. It mattered little what she was saying. He was completely bewitched.

Pouring a clear liquid into a tiny, delicate china cup, she handed it to him before pouring another for herself. Looking at him with her dark imploring eyes, she tapped the rim of her cup to his and nodded that he should drink.

The wine was warm, potent, yet unlike the dark rum he was used to, this drink slipped like satin down his throat. He wondered what it was as Jun refilled their cups.

Jun looked to his side, then gave a quick frown. Looking at him, she gestured writing. Will lifted a shoulder and shook his head. He hadn't brought along the slate. Without it, he'd not have to answer any questions— or avoid any—that might incriminate him. Dinner would be dinner, not an inquisition. As the wine lit a warming path through his limbs, Will was confident they'd manage without it.

He began to relax. Not having the slate put him at the advantage, as well. Reading people was a honed skill, he'd been doing it all his life. And Jun was easy to read when she was like this. As if coming through that door had also pulled back a curtain. This was the true Jian Jun. Surprising as the beauty of these surroundings was, it gave him another layer of knowledge about her. The armor she wore during the day not only covered and protected her body. It also hid much of her emotions. But here in this garden, she'd lowered the shield enough to let him glimpse inside the fortress she had so expertly built for herself, to find the essence of the woman.

As Jun offered him food from the banquet before him, he wondered how many she had allowed into her personal sanctuary. He noted the tiniest of tremors in her hand as she filled his plate. He smiled. Her nerves gave her away. Entertaining men in her garden was not a common occurrence.

Will signed *'Thank you,'* and waited until she settled with her own food to begin eating. The aroma of the food made his mouth water. Over the last few days, he'd eaten little. His belly had begun to protest.

Jun lifted two long, jade sticks from the table and used them to bring a tidbit of food to her mouth. He'd seen this method of eating before, but had never been called to use it himself. Without his knife, however, short of using his hands like a barbarian, the twin lengths of jade were his only option.

He held both sticks in his hand and watched her for a moment before attempting the maneuver himself. Looked simple enough. You merely pinched the food with the jade and held it while bringing it to your mouth. Easy. After several fumbled attempts, however, he set the blasted things aside in frustration before his anger got the better of him and forced him to snap the thin lengths of jade in half. Was this an eastern form of torture? His belly mumbled its displeasure.

If he couldn't eat, he could certainly lift his glass. He poured himself more wine before meeting Jun's questioning glance. Jun set aside her own utensils before sliding closer to him and picking up his. Lifting her hand, she set one of the sticks in the crook between her first finger and her thumb and showed him how the second length of jade moved against the first. To demonstrate she picked up a tender bit of beef and fed it to him.

The intimacy of that simple act sent a different hunger through Will. He held Jun's gaze as he savored the rich flavor of the meat and unique spices until she broke the heated connection to watch his throat work.

She was so close. Kissably close. To hell with the food, there was only one thing he was desperate to taste. Will took the jade sticks from her hand and once again set them aside. Jun followed his every move before returning the warmth of her gaze to his.

Will ran the tip of his finger along the smooth line of her jaw before catching the tip of her chin and lifting her face up to meet his. Moving to within a hair's breadth between them, Will caught a low movement in the ferns behind Jun.

Cursing his lack of weapon for the twentieth time today, he surged to one side, roughly pulling Jun behind him. He snatched the jade from the table and held it aloft like a pick. It wouldn't kill her attacker, but it would stop them long enough to get her away.

Jun scrambled to her feet behind him. He held his other arm wide to block her. Keeping her safely behind him until she slipped beneath his arm. She pushed one hand to the middle of his chest and gave a shove to stop him while she grasped her other hand around his wrist, holding his arm high.

He pulled his arm out of her hold. *What the bloody hell are you doing? Damn it woman, I'm trying to defend you.*

Will then saw a child emerge from beneath the planting. Wide eyed and mischievous, she peered at him behind a tangle of dark curls. He retreated in an instant. His heart fisting blood through his veins. The rush of adrenaline flooding him screeched into reverse. Will dropped the jade to the table as if it scorched his fingers.

Jun caught the child by the scruff of her neck as the imp tried to scoot by and shook an angry finger at the young girl's nose. She pointed sternly toward the outer rooms and sent the child on her way with a firm tap to her behind. The girl rushed a few paces then stopped to look back at them with a clever smile. Jun frowned at her and pointed again.

Ting appeared out of nowhere and scooped the little one into her arms. Fussing and bowing, she rushed the child away.

Will's breathing hadn't quite returned to normal, but his thoughts raced like a gale. Who was that? Was she Jun's daughter? Maybe that was the reason for the marked difference in Jun's character. On one side of the door she was a warrior, on the other a mother. Did the child explain her drive to build her vast empire? And more importantly, did it alter the way he was feeling about her? Children were a rarity in his life. They were landlocked bits of a future he never considered. He wasn't sure he'd consider them now.

Will's gaze traveled over Jun's body again. If the child belonged to her, what would it matter? *Damn it.* He wished to hell he had the writing slate now.

Chapter 11

Jun turned and shook her head, holding a steadying hand to her throat. She didn't know which had thrown her off balance more. Qi scaring the wits out of both of them, or coming so close to kissing Will. Both were making her heart flutter like a bird trapped in her chest.

Will still stood next to the table. In his gallant rush to put her behind him, half their dinner now littered the ground and their seats. Standing with his hands on his hips, the cross-over of his shirt bowed open. She couldn't help but be mesmerized by the rise and fall of his strong chest.

"I'm sorry." Jun held her arms wide, before looking away. She indicated Qi and Ting's path. "Qi is s a handful at times, but she has a loving heart." Why was she talking? To hear herself? Jun bit her lip to cease her rambling.

When she looked back at him, Will pointed at the path, as well, then back to her in question. He held his arms as if he cradled a baby, and gestured toward her again. Did he think Qi was her child?

Jun shook her head and waved her hands in front of her. "No, she is not mine."

Will nodded that he understood. She couldn't tell if he was relieved or disappointed somehow.

A familiar twinge pricked at her heart. Not that she didn't love Qi like her own. She and Fu had always planned to have children one day. During the first years of their marriage, Jun had made sure she took precautions to prevent an untimely pregnancy. She'd been trained well at the Painted Palace, after all. What she couldn't prevent, however, was her husband's untimely death. More than losing Fu, she had lost the dream of having children together. It was one of the reasons Qi had become so dear to her. How did she begin to explain all that to Will with simple hand gestures and nods of her head? Damn it, she wished to hell she had the writing slate.

Jun straightened her dress and finished composing herself. As much as she longed to turn the clock back to those tender moments before Will had thought they were being ambushed, perhaps fate had been the one to save her.

She hadn't been thinking clearly all day. Her body's neglected passions were betraying her with its waves of ridiculous desires. It wasn't like her to lose control. Not over a man. No matter how handsome Captain Quinn might be. And she was above using seduction to get her the information she wanted from him. Given her years of thievery and pillaging, it was odd, but Jun wanted him to trust her.

Will bent and started to clear up the mess littering the flat stones paving the archway. Jun rushed to stop him. "No, please… You needn't do that." She tugged on his arm until he straightened. Looking over the table, she hoped to salvage their evening until Will used the tip of his finger to once more turn her face toward him.

He wore such a serious look. Giving her a short bow, he then stood tall, placed a fist over his heart and made a small circle. Jun was at a loss as to what that meant, but before she could figure it out, he turned and left the garden.

"Wait," Jun called after his retreating back. "You're yelling at a deaf man, you idiot," she scolded herself. "Wait…" she whispered. Exasperated she sat and kicked at the spoiled food. "Damn."

* * * *

Will moved through the dim corridors and returned to the sweltering sanctuary of his paper-walled room. He slid the door closed behind him. If ever he truly needed the satisfaction of feeling a door slam into its framing, this would have been it. The gentle slide of the paper door made him consider putting his fist through the delicate painted panel.

What the hell had he been thinking? A refined dinner with a beautiful, desirable woman? He could capture a ship and strip her of every last bit of bounty in less time than it took for him to make a complete and utter fool out of himself tonight.

There was a reason he didn't tarry with women. Spend time in their company for anything other than a few hours of hedonistic sexual play? Impossible. He was a bloody pirate, not some refined gentleman with lace and ruffles. Even if he could speak words aloud, he didn't know the first thing about polite chatter.

Will lifted the forgotten slate from where he had strategically left it. Truth be told it wasn't interrogation he was leery of, it was the bloody pleasantries. Pure syrupy puke. *Oh my dearest, what a lovely shade of blue you're wearing. It reminds me of the color of a dead man's face. And dinner is delicious. Have you ever tried roasted bilge rat?* Will tossed the slate back on the bed in anger. *Shite and piddle!*

And the child... Bloody hell, he could have killed the child with a blasted stick? There was one thing to be thankful about for not having his weapons. Had he been wearing a blade, he would have slashed through the foliage and killed that wee babe before he even saw her.

Will dropped to the edge of his bed and ran a weary hand over his eyes. What the bloody hell was he thinking? That he was going to seduce a woman like Jian Jun? She was hardly some lusty pepper merchant's daughter. She was bloody Jian Jun.

And yet, she had him under her spell. Luring him into her exotic net. Feeding him delicious food, plying him with strong wine. How else do you explain the flash of disappointment at learning that child was not hers? When had he *ever* wanted children? Where did that thought even come from? He was a fucking pirate!

And she was off-with-his-head, hang-him-by-his-nuts *Jian Jun!* One glimpse of pale breast and he'd lost his mind.

He stood and began to pace and scraped a hand over his face. Truth was, he hadn't thought clearly since he hit the blasted water during the storm. He had to get off this island before he did something he'd truly regret. After tonight's fiasco, the sooner the better. Back to the sea where he didn't feel like a fish flapping on the damn beach.

Speaking of beach, Will stopped his pacing and glanced toward the hank of bright red that had once been the proud sail of the *Scarlet Night.* He crossed the room and felt its edge. Almost dry. He needed to finish this. It was time. He'd put off his duty long enough.

Pulling the piece to the floor he retrieved the ink and quill from the table near his bed. The nib of the quill caught on the coarse weave of the canvas as he began to write, and the black of the ink spread in an ugly blot after each dip, but it mattered little. What mattered was that he remembered each and every name of his crew and added it to the cloth. All forty-three names.

Fm. Captain, Alice Louise Tupper Quinn, First Mate, Richard Griffin, Helmsman, Oliver Hills, Quartermaster, Alfred Higgins...

One after another he added each name to the fabric of the sail until they filled the space. He could see each face in his memory.

Later he'd repeat the same list when he made the final entry in the ship's log. He pulled the books from their hiding place and ran his fingers over the silvered corners before tucking them away again. Will checked the log box under the bed. No one had disturbed it.

With no lock on the door, he'd be daft to leave his logs in a box with no workable hasp. Instead, he moved the incriminating log books into the straw padding of the mattress and filled the box with stones.

It wasn't a perfect solution. However, he'd learned a few tricks over the years. Strategically placed bits of thread. A strand of hair set across a door frame. Invisible ways of knowing straight away if someone had entered a room before him, picked a certain lock. Rummaged through his belongings. A pre-warning of sorts that had saved his neck on more than one occasion.

Will set his pre-warnings again as he left his room for the second time that night. With the square of sail folded under his arm, he made his way through the empty corridors. He'd memorized the safest way out of the grand palace earlier in the day and soon was skirting the village and making his way to the north beach once again.

The tide was high, but heading out. Will waded into the warm dark waters, soaking him to mid-thigh. Unfolding the sail, he laid it on top of the waves. A waning moon gave enough light to see the waters take hold of the canvas, seeping once more into each strand. Darkening the red to the color of blood before the pull of the waves plucked it from his fingers and carried it from him.

He pulled a deep breath into his lungs as he watched it float away. In his mind, Will said the final words necessary to honor his lost crew:

I, William Quinn, being the Captain and sole survivor of the proud ship known to us as the Scarlet Night *do commit the bodies of these forty-three souls to the deep until the day of the resurrection when the sea shall give up her dead and we shall sail together once again.*

Will stood there a long time. Long after the sail had been pulled under the surface of the water. Lost to his memories. Numb in a hailstorm of brutal emotions. Would he ever be rid of this burning sense of guilt and grief?

He ran a thumb over the face of Tupper's ring and twisted it on his finger. Damn it, he could use a stiff drink, or five, or twenty, but without a coin to his name, that wasn't going to happen. All he had was this ring. His thumb worried the hole in the gold. One day soon, he vowed to replace its lost pearl.

Once he got back to being a proper captain, of course, doing what he did best. Standing at the helm of his own ship, spurring his crew into battle, swinging his cutlass, ordering the guns to fire, filling his coffers. He could still smell the sulfur bite of cannon smoke and the tang of blood in the air. Feel the powerful ride of the ship beneath his boots, and the vibration of the rigging as the *Scarlet Night* raced along the tips of the waves. What he missed most was the first breath. Like a babe being born. The pull of pure air into your lungs after leaving the docks and harbors behind with the bow of the ship leading you into open water. That first glorious breath of clean sea air. He would stand with Tupper in the bow...

Will slammed his mind shut against the memory. The pain of losing her was still too raw for him. He trailed his fingers through the water as he resigned himself to the next chapter of his life until an idea washed over him. Time to weigh anchor and get back to whatever life had stretched out before him. He needed a new bow to stand upon. The sea was calling.

Leaving the surf, Will headed back into town. He'd noticed two or three taverns doing a fair business as he passed by. Perhaps his luck at the card tables hadn't gone down with the ship.

Entering one he walked through the crowded bar toward the gaming rooms in the back and slapped Tupper's ring on the table as his buy-in stake in one of the games. Collateral of sorts.

Don't worry, Tupper. I'm not about to lose it. I promise this will be the one and only time it leaves my hand.

Several hours later, true to his promise, Will stood away from the table and pushed Tupper's ring back onto his finger. Adjusting wide leather straps to his frame, he fit his new baldric and pistol over his head. The last owner was a much smaller man, but he was gracious enough to leave Will his extra shot and powder in the bargain. A boarding sword now hung from Will's belt, as well. It was far too light but it would do until he found a better blade. Had his companions not begun to question his winning streak, he'd have cleared the table, but greed was never one of Will's vices. One fat purse would do—for a start.

Will stopped at the bar on his way out and dropped a handful of coins on its polished surface. He pointed behind the bartender at the two bottles of fine rum he wanted.

Stepping once more into the night, Will pulled the cork of one with his teeth. He raised the bottle to the heavens in salute before pouring a healthy measure onto the ground. A drink for the dead. Then he poured a healthier measure down his parched throat. The sweet burn of the rum into his belly fueling his resolve. No satined wine in tiny cups for him. Rum was his drink. Pirating was his life. It was high time he got back to it.

Two guards eyed him as he reentered the palace but did nothing to stop him, or even question him. Not that he would have...or more to the point, *could have* answered them. And it wasn't because the rum was doing a fine job in quenching his thirst. He handed one guard an empty bottle and slapped the shoulder of the other.

Pulling the cork from the second bottle, he took another swallow. Damn, card play was thirsty work.

He only got lost once heading back to his room, but still had his head enough to check for unwanted visitors. The inconspicuous bit of thread was exactly where he'd left it.

Will glanced back down the dim corridor and wrinkled his nose. The man who was charged with following him reeked of pickled cabbage. He'd caught his scent before they'd left the palace. The bloke did a fine job and kept his cover. Will never saw him, but he didn't have to. The man's smell could knock a buzzard off a dead man.

Will removed his newly won weapons, flopped down on the bed, and closed his eyes. Without the ship's lanterns to tell him, he had no clue as to the time. Lanterns were one consolation made to him on the *Scarlet*. When the timekeeper rang the bells, he lit the corresponding lanterns for Will. That and the use of the bright warning flags in the crow's nest and the finest crew that ever sailed, eliminated any interference with his running of the ship. The crew learned his simple signals. His lead officers watched for them and passed the orders silently through the ranks. Sounds of the battle, pistols firing, cannons blasting, the war cries of the men, never got in the way of his commands.

Aye...they were a fine lot, his blasted crew. The best there be. Will took another drink and tossed an arm over his eyes. He should write the last log post, now that he had performed the commitment of their souls to the sea. It wasn't like him to shirk his responsibility, but the bed was comfortable and the rum was dark and sweet...

And a great part of him would rather lie there and think about the long-haired, almond-eyed Jun. God, he wanted to kiss her. Pull her into his arms and sate his curious longing once and for all. He wondered if she would take his head if he slipped back into her rooms to do just that. Will ran a hand over his throat and cocked an eyebrow at the sudden interest of his cock.

Might be well worth it.

He took another swig of his rum and held the bottle to his chest. Aye, it would definitely be worth it.

Chapter 12

Jun signed off on the accountings from three of her largest ships. Her scribes rolled the long parchments. "The latest captures are not up to the standards for these crews," she pointed out to Peng. "What excuse do they give?"

"The Chinese Emperor has increased the efforts of his fleet to capture us and end our control of these seas. The waters are becoming exceedingly guarded."

"But my fleet is more powerful." Jun nodded to her accountants and dismissed them.

"Aye, but we are spread too wide. The Imperial fleet is concentrating all its efforts to our south, blocking our ships from attacking the merchants heading into the strait. Our junks have been forced to patrol different waters. That is why it is so important we make the push farther to the west."

"I agree, but we've been reckless in our travels around the Cape of Good Hope in the past. We can't afford to spread our reach if we lose our fingers in the process."

Jun scanned the great hall beyond Peng's shoulder. It was the tenth time she had done so since she arrived. She was looking for him. *Will.* Jun gave herself a mental shake. Why did it matter so much if he was there or he wasn't? She had more important things to concern herself with. Her traitorous eyes made another quick glance about the room.

Foolish woman. How many times must I replay the scene in my mind?

So he'd almost kissed her…didn't…then left as if his trousers were on fire. It meant nothing. He was but one man. She was a woman of the world. Ruled thousands. She had been treated far worse by far better. It truly only stung her pride if she thought about it.

And she'd thought about it all night.

Forcing herself to stay on the task before her, Jun resisted the relentless urge to seek him out. What would she even say to him? His actions relayed his feelings quite well. There was no need for him to write it out on a bit of slate. No need for discussion. It was wise to stop things before anything started. He could have saved them both from... from what?

Knowing what it would be like to have his lips on hers? The sweep of his touch? The taste of his mouth? The press of his body along hers. In hers.

Stop! Her body pulsed with want.

Jun straightened her spine and set her jaw. She was certain she would survive without such an added complication in her life right now. It was a good thing that nothing had transpired between them. So be it. End of story. She'd already lost too many nights' sleep over the man. Enough was enough.

When had she become such a liar?

Concentrating again on the manifests before her, a flush of warmth sent delicious tingles over her skin. Jun didn't have to look up from her work to somehow know when Will entered the hall. Her stomach fluttered behind her breastplate alerting her to his presence.

"Do you wish to know where your Captain Quinn spent most of last night?" Peng asked.

Against her will, she lifted her chin and was surprised by Will's more rugged appearance as he moved through the morning's crowd.

"Where did he get those weapons?" Will sported a new baldric holding a long-barreled pistol and a side hung sword. Under one arm, he carried his writing slate, a leather book with silver adorned corners, and his quill.

"He had a busy evening," said Peng. He leaned closer. The tip of his beard brushed her arm. "My man reported him leaving the palace last night and heading first to the beach. There wasn't much of a moon to illuminate his exact movements, but he waded out several yards then spread a large square of cloth on the water. He remained out there for quite a while before returning to shore."

Jun couldn't take her eyes from him. "That's doesn't answer my question. Did the pistol float to him on a wave?"

"I was getting to that," insisted Peng. "After leaving the beach, he made his way back to the village and visited one of the taverns where he used the gold ring he wears to buy his way into a game of cards with some other men." Peng pointed a long finger in Will's direction. "It's their weapons he wears now."

Jun's eyebrows pushed toward her headdress. "He won them gambling?"

"Aye." Peng scowled and crossed his arms over his chest. "Didn't lose a single hand."

"Do you suspect he cheated?"

Peng shook his head. "If he did, he's the best there be. I'm told they changed decks three times. He never interfered with the dealer. The other players were not unskilled, and yet, I understand he played with an unwavering intensity. Refused to fold. Called every bluff."

Jun was coming to know that intensity first hand. How was it, he appeared bigger now that he was armed? More impressive. Will carried the weapons as if he were born to them. It gave him a dangerous edge she found staggering. "Perhaps he's just lucky."

Peng snorted. "Well, his luck can't hold out forever. We'll soon hear back from my queries amongst the fleet. If there's anything interesting to learn about Captain Quinn, we shall have the information within the week. Until then, he is allowed to come and go as he pleases, but I've informed those ships in the harbor that they are not to take him on without your order. Until we know he isn't part of a wider threat—"

Jun shot an angry glare at Peng. "My order? When did *I* give this order?"

"I simply thought—"

"You *think* what I tell you to think. And you only give orders that I give. That is the way it has been since my husband's reign of this fleet, and how it will continue to be. Of late, you seem to forget this simple law."

The muscle in Peng's jaw twitched. He lowered his voice. "And it is because I served so faithfully under the command of your husband that I ask you to trust my guidance in this matter. Have I ever given you cause to doubt my allegiance? Doubt my loyalty to you or this empire? Have you ever witnessed me serving my own interests? Everything I do, I do for you and you alone. I remain your humble servant in all things."

Jun released an angry breath. It was true. Peng had never shown her anything but his devotion to her. Still, there was something in his insistence that pricked at her. "And I rely on your loyalty, Chou Peng. You're correct, you have served me well. Sometimes, too well." After a quick glance toward Will, Jun conceded. "The order shall stand as given."

Peng stepped off the dais and bowed before departing the hall with several of his officers. Jun followed their exit. Perhaps it was her growing interest in Will Peng was sensing and reacting to, but still there was a stream of underlying tension between her and her first mate which had never been there before. A testing of limits. A quiet rebelliousness she'd not witnessed from him.

Or perhaps it was her own rebellious feelings? Had she cloistered herself away for too long? Served her duties to the detriment of her desires as a woman? It would explain the erratic swing of her moods.

Jun glanced at Captain Quinn again and raised an eyebrow to the rush of heat that followed. She should follow Peng and thank him. After all, because of him, Will wouldn't be leaving Pandang any time soon. At least not without her permission.

Dipping her quill, Jun scribbled a quick note and caught the attention of Ting.

"Bring this to Captain Quinn," she instructed. "Be discreet." Jun lowered her voice to a whisper. "I wish to meet with him in the gardens. Bring him there. Ask him to wait for me."

"Yes, mistress." Ting took the note.

"And, Ting," Jun added as she handed her a coin. "Take Qi into the village for the afternoon. Enjoy a day beyond these walls. Buy her a small treat."

"You mustn't spoil her, mistress."

"Let me, just this once." Jun smiled.

"That is what you say each time." Ting shook her head.

Jun waved her away. "It is my only indulgence."

"I shall pick up the new qi pao you ordered from the tailor, and be back in time for the evening meal." Ting insisted.

"Thank you, but there is no rush. Take your time. It is a beautiful day." Jun watched Ting deliver her note to Will and looked away when he turned his gaze toward her. Then cursed herself for behaving like some shy schoolgirl.

This constant questioning in her mind, the heated rushes at every thought of him, and the replay of last night's scene, it was becoming too much of a distraction.

If Will shared a measure of her feelings, Jun wanted to know. If he didn't, then she could move on. Put it behind her where it belonged. Hell, if that were the case, she'd grant him leave on any ship he fancied, banish him from her shores, and forget she ever learned his name.

Out of the corner of her eye, Jun followed Ting and Will as they moved beyond the bevy of people in the hall. It took all her self-control not to rush off the dais to join him.

Soon Ting and Qi passed by her, hand in hand, on their way to the village. An excited flutter skipped over Jun's skin. He waited for her. Alone.

Jun took another few agonizingly slow moments before she rose and, feigning a casual posture, retreated to her private quarters. At first, she didn't see him. Had he refused her request and left without her notice? But then she caught a glimpse of his dark head as he strolled through the gardens.

Pulling the heavy leather-plate armor from her, she ran a smoothing hand over her hair before heading out to meet him. A cool breeze fluttered the thin silk of her under blouse across her heated flesh and chilled her nipples into firm peaks. The only other sound was the heels of her boots crunching along the shelled pathway and the ever-present trickle of water into the ponds.

Jun smiled to herself as she indulged in a stolen moment to privately admire the span of Will's shoulders and the long fall of his hair. The addition of the baldric and sword emphasized the play of his muscles across his back and draped seductively off one hip to enhance the high, firm curve of his a—

Will turned and caught her ogling him. The corner of his mouth tipped into a grin. In return he swept her with a heated gaze down the full length of her body and back again, ogling a bit of his own. The firmness of her nipples was not due to a chill anymore. Quite the opposite. She was aflame.

Part of her wanted to rush into his arms, and part of her wanted to sing at the top of her lungs. Whatever his reasoning for rushing off last night, it had nothing to do with a lack of interest on his part.

He held her gaze and erased any doubts she may have had.

Jun reached out her hand to him, which he took with no hesitation. She led him back to the same alcove as last night. All evidence of their spoiled evening had been cleared away.

Releasing Will's hand, she took care to place the two cushions they'd used back in the exact placement from hours before. She knelt as she had been, and indicated that he join her.

Will placed the book and slate he still carried onto the table along with his baldric and sword before sitting. Jun's breathing rose under the intensity of his stare. She snatched the writing stone from the table and simply wrote:

Where were we?

Chapter 13

Where were we?

Will remembered exactly where they had been. The scene had been on a constant loop through his thoughts since the moment he walked away last night. Through everything that went on in the past hours, he hadn't been able to lose the image of them here.

Gone was the rich embroidery of her dress, but in its place the gossamer-thin silk of her top suited him fine. Even in the close leather of her trousers and boots, she was nothing but feminine and breathtakingly lovely.

Will reached over and slipped the long braid of her hair over her shoulder and proceeded to unfasten the length of leather that secured the end. With gentle care, he unplaited her hair until he could run his fingers through its dark, shiny length.

He circled his face with a single gesture. *'Beautiful.'*

As he'd done last night, he traced the fine line of her jaw with a fingertip before tipping her chin and lowering his mouth to hers.

Here. We were right here.

Will covered her lips with his own and caught her sigh as she opened her mouth to him. She tasted so sweet. Just as he'd imagined. Will pushed his hand back into her hair to cradle her head as he slanted his kiss in the opposite direction. Jun's eyes fluttered closed as the kiss deepened. She slipped her hand up the inside of his shirt before winding an arm around his neck and leaning the softness of her body tight against his.

Will caught the gentle moan from her throat and began to pull away, but Jun tightened her hold on him and brought his mouth back to hers.

In response, Will slipped an arm about her waist and tugged her into his lap. Jun pulled away. Their breathing came fast as Will searched her eyes for some signal. Some sign as to whether he'd rushed her, been too bold. Some indication as to what she wanted. Had he been a fumbling idiot yet again?

He waited. Didn't move a single muscle, although his heart worked overtime to pound blood to his increasingly painful erection. He reined his base urge to take her right there and then. Jun was not the kind of woman he was used to being with. He was in foreign territory in every bloody sense of the word.

But then she lowered her gaze to his mouth and ran a feather-light touch of a single fingertip to outline the lower edge of his lip. She dropped a tiny kiss there before trailing her touch down the front of his throat. Dipping her head she kissed him there as well.

Will held himself taut. Even when she nipped the sensitive skin where his neck swept into his shoulder. His cock surged in his trousers. If she were trying to kill him, she was doing a fine job of it.

He wanted to tear her clothing away and lay her down amongst the ferns, but he was at her mercy. Then Jun lifted his hand from where it idled at her waist, and placed his palm over the sweet curve of her breast before taking his mouth again.

Bloody hell.

Touching the soft silk of her blouse was nothing compared to feel of the satined skin that lay beneath. The roughness of his hands caught at the delicate fabric as she arched into his touch, reminding him that he was nothing but a time-hardened sea thief, and she was a queen.

Rocking her hips as she pressed the pebbled tip of her breast against his palm, the movement atop the ridge of his erection nearly sent him over the edge.

Her lips moved on his. She was saying something to him between kisses. Urging him on? Begging him to stop? Go faster? Slow down?

Frustration welled in him. He pulled back and searched her face. His breathing matched hers and fluttered the fine hair at her temples. A bright blush tinged her cheeks. His kisses had rouged her lips.

'Beautiful.' He signed again. *'Stunning.'*

Jun cradled his cheek. A small frown knit the dark curve of her eyebrows as her chest continued to rise and fall beneath his hand.

She spoke again. He watched her mouth, desperate for the instant ability to read her lips. Instead, he released her and eased what little Jun's hold on him would allow. Reaching to the side he retrieved the slate.

I need to know what you're saying. He hastily scratched over the surface of the stone.

Jun gently took it from his hands. *I want to know what YOU are saying.*

She mimicked the sign he had made.

I'm telling you, you're beautiful.

A small smile lifted the corners of her mouth. *Thank you,* she wrote.

Will tapped the slate and made the sign for *'Thank you.'*

She repeated the movement. Practicing, *'Beautiful'. 'Thank you.'* Then her name. Then his.

What is this? She wrote, before putting a closed fist to her chest and making a circle. *You did this last night.*

It means, I'm sorry, Will replied.

Her frown returned. *You did nothing to feel sorry about.*

Ruined our evening.

She shook her head in disagreement.

Will rubbed against the slate. *Who was the child?*

Qi. Ting is her mother. They passed the stone back and forth between them, scrubbing it clean and jotting down their thoughts.

Her father is not Chinese.

Jun nodded. *He fled the British several years ago. He now works for me.* She rubbed away the words. *Qi is a special child. Simple.*

It was Will's turn to frown.

Jun continued. *But her heart is kind and she is 'Beautiful.'* She proudly signed the last word.

Will ran the back of his finger over the gentle curve of her cheek before writing, *Not near as lovely as you.*

Jun signed *'Thank you'* before she lowered her gaze and stroked the edge of his shirt.

The heated fever of their kisses hadn't cooled. Only mellowed into something less desperate, more enduring. The attraction was still there but had coupled with an equal desire to know one another. Where others had treated Will as a curiosity, a novelty, Jun actually seemed to care about learning who he was and how to communicate with him.

Will held her gaze for a long moment before he erased the slate once more and asked her, *What are we doing?*

Giving a small smile, Jun lifted her shoulders in a shrug. She curved the side of her body to lean against him and continued to stroke the planes of his chest. The warmth and weight of her brought an unusual calm to him. A healing balm for his battered soul. As if she were exactly where she belonged and his question didn't need an answer.

Will kissed the top of her head and breathed in the light scent of her. They stayed tangled up in one another for a long while.

Jun was the first to move. She picked up the slate. *Stay?*

Was she asking him to stay for the day? The night? A week? For all time? A few more minutes holding her in his arms, he might answer yes to all of them.

She added, *I still owe you dinner.*

Will shook his head. He tipped his chin toward his things still on the table. *Need to finish my work. Came to the hall seeking more ink.*

Work here. Quiet. Peaceful. No one will bother you. She laid a gentle kiss on his mouth. *I have duties as well. Wait for me.* Jun kissed him again. This time, her mouth lingered, opened to the slow sweep of his tongue, and was quick to fan the flames of their earlier heat. She eased away and held the slate insistently tapping under her last words, *Wait for me,* then added the word, *Please.*

Will took her hand from his chest and placed it palm down on hers then moved her hand in a circle. He tapped the slate and repeated the motion. *'Please'*

Jun repeated the motion, imploring him with her eyes. *'Please?'*

How could he say no? Will nodded and was graced with her smile. An earth-shattering, breath-taking smile. Raise the white flag, he surrendered, and yet, was it surrender when every inch of his body told him he'd won?

Standing in the garden holding a jar of ink, Will watched Jun make the transformation from pliant heated woman in his arms back into the battle-hardened empress. Still tasting her passion on his lips, it was hard for him to think of her any other way, but the truth of it was right there.

As she finished replaiting her hair and donned the last bit of armor, her conversion was complete, and with a quick glance in his direction, Jun passed through the door separating her two distinctly different lives once more.

Will pulled a deep breath into his lungs, ran a hand over the roughness of his jaw, and tried to process all that had happened. What the hell was he doing? Dropping his hand to his hip, Will closed his eyes and hung his head. He knew damn well what he was doing. He was losing his heart. Again.

He shifted his shoulders. The pull of the scars on his back reminded him of the last time he'd given away his heart and what that had cost him. This time...no, this time was different. When Bump fell for Samantha Christian, he gave away his foolish heart knowing nothing would come of it. Sam cared for him, yes, but as a friend. She never shared his feelings.

With Jun, the winds had shifted.

Will lifted his head and looked around. He moved to the low table and set the ink next to his log book. Moving the scattered cushions back to where they started, he sat down to work, but couldn't stop his mind from churning.

He picked up the quill and twirled the feather between his fingers before tossing it aside in frustration. This was ridiculous. He was no child. Neither was he a fool, but with matters of the heart and understanding the workings of a woman's mind… He was lost and adrift in murky seas.

One thing was certain, however. Will shifted his weight on the cushion. If Jun wanted only what other woman from his past had wanted, this stiff ache in his crotch would be gone, and he'd be searching for his blasted pants among the potted plants by now with no hope of ever seeing her again.

Damn it, this *was* different. And it was like trying to find his direction in a bloody hurricane. Glancing at the log book, he scoffed, *We all know how good I am at doing that.*

Will lifted the ornate silver latch and opened the log book to his last entry. *With fair winds and following seas, our route runs true and our rum be plentiful. Respectfully submitted this seventeenth day of August, in the year of our Lord…*

He ran his fingers over his signature. Would he ever be rid of the crushing heaviness in his chest? It had been near a week since his final entry. Seven days and an entire lifetime.

Will stared at the following empty page and thumbed through each empty page after that. This couldn't be the end. How could it all just stop? Unfortunately he was the only one who could answer that question. Swallowing the bitter lump in his throat, he dipped his quill and began his last and final entry:

On Wednesday, the eighteenth day of August, in the year of our Lord seventeen hundred and seventeen, the ship known to all as the Scarlet Night *was lost in heavy seas and high winds while navigating through the Strait of Malacca due north of the Brothers Islands of Pandang and Salahnama.*

All hands were lost. Save one…

Will recounted each horrific moment. Each scene that would forever be etched in his mind. As with the sail, he scribed each and every name of his lost crew and recounted the events to the best of his memory.

He blew across the wet ink and waited until it was dry to close the book. Holding it in his lap, he ran his thumb over the salt-stain that marred its once pristine cover. Perhaps he should add the words *The End* to the last page in some flourished script. The thought cause his stomach to turn.

Leaning his head back, Will closed his eyes and breathed in the rich smells of Jun's garden and tried to forget. He could see why she created this sanctuary. It was easy to imagine it as some protected cocoon where nothing dark or sinister could reach.

When Will opened his eyes, the child, Qi, stood watching him with a wide-eyed curiosity. He straightened in his seat, and nodded to her in greeting. She didn't move, yet held him with her stare.

Jun had mentioned Qi was simple. Not developed in her mind. Will didn't want to frighten the wee girl, so he made no move himself. It was a standoff to see which of them would look away first.

Then the child dashed away. Like the darting of a fish. She was back as quickly as she had left, hugging a scrap of filthy cloth. Its original color or purpose a true mystery.

Qi grabbed one corner of the second cushion at the table and dragged it around the ends of his outstretched legs, pulling it close to his before settling herself next to him.

With raised eyebrows, he peered down at the child. She, in turn, blinked up at him with clear wide eyes that spoke of her father's western heritage, as well as the riotous curls that tangled in an unruly mess about her head. An innocent grin curved the gentle pink of her lips.

Will had always taken a small measure of pride in the fact that he made a rather intimidating presence with his height and appearance, but this child was not fearful at all. Quite the opposite, judging by the eager, expectant look on her little face. Did she think she'd found herself a new friend?

He shook his head at her. *I don't know what you want, little one, but you won't find it here. You should run away. I'm a nasty old pirate.*

Qi then reached out her small hand and patted the log before snuggling in closer to him. Will froze. If the mysteries of women baffled him, the workings of children were as foreign to him as the landscape of the moon. Qi tapped at the book harder.

Was she wanting him to read her a story? A bedtime fairytale?

No, child. Will shook his head and shrugged. *'Sorry.'*

Qi frowned and tugged the book from his grasp. Lifting the cover, she turned each page. She kept shaking her head. Turning the pages faster and faster as if she were searching for something. She pushed the book back into Will's hands and rushed to the boarder of flat stones that accentuated the pathway through the garden. The child crouched and patted a chalked drawing there of some creature with stick legs and huge eyes.

And then she was back at his side, patting his logbook.

Child, I don't have any idea... Did she want him to draw pictures? Of course, she wanted it to be a picture book.

The corner of Will's mouth tipped at the thought. An illustrated log would give the poor little chit nightmares. He looked down at her again and shook his head no again.

Her only reaction was to purse her lower lip and give him a look of disappointment. She settled back, huffed a breath and tipped her head to rest it against him. She hooked her arm through his.

What in the bloody hell—he stopped. Even in his mind, it wasn't right to curse in front of a child. Especially not little girls. The press of her small body warmed his arm. Short of shoving her aside, he was at a loss as to how to remove her. She was attached to him like a blasted barnacle to a hull and showed no signs of leaving. Only an evil bastard would shake her off like a mangy dog would a flea.

So, he waited. Why not, he reasoned. She wasn't causing any harm. It wasn't as if he were heading anywhere. They could wait for Jun together. She'd know what to do with the child.

Will peeked down at Qi. Her eyes were closed. The rise and fall of her chest was slow and steady. Was she sleeping? *Son of a b—*

All he could do was shake his head. He leaned back and closed his own eyes, fighting a smirk. If Tupper could see him now…

The crushing ache returned. Perhaps it would forever hurt to think about her. About all of them.

Now there were stories to tell. Talk about bedtime tales and picture books. Years of one adventure after another. He looked down at the curly top of the child's head before closing his eyes once more. Oh wee one, if only I could tell you about their escapades, but all the accounts lay at the bottom of the sea. Will's eyes snapped open. He sat forward, and lifted his logbook once more, flipping through the pages of impersonal facts and events. It was unfortunate that they didn't tell the whole story—the story he'd been a silent witness to for close to thirty years.

He looked at the sweetness of Qi's innocent face. She'd never learn about the grand journeys of the *Scarlet Night.* No one would, yet Will remembered them all.

The night of a fierce storm when Will had been little more than Qi's age, when Tupper braved the crashing seas and bucking masts to climb the center rigging to untangle a bunt line. Or the time Ric 'Ricochet' Robbins had earned his nickname with one perfect shot of a cannon.

If anyone was to know, he'd need to write it all down. Who else would there be to do it? Tell their tales? Carry on the legend?

Will remembered everything. Everyone. That disgusting beast of a Scot, MacTavish, who smelled like an old sheep dipped in shite and sulphur. The strong quiet dignity of Gavin Quinn and the horrific day when Will watched him die as Port Royal, Jamaica was swallowed into the sea. Samantha coming aboard with her chopped hair and soot-smeared face trying to pass as a lad. Or the look on those British Navy bastards' faces when Will and Tupper tied them naked to a dock, their bollocks swinging in the breeze while they stole back the *Scarlet Night* and escaped into an inky sea.

He looked down at Qi again. *Maybe I'll let ye read that one when yer a might older.*

There were still plenty of empty pages in this logbook. Recalling the stories, immortalizing them for all time, might be the reason he was still breathing. The reason he was spared. To write it all down so the *Scarlet Night* wouldn't be lost. She could sail forever in the pages of a book.

Why that's a mighty fine idea, little one. Might even find a bloke to draw a picture or two, just for you. Will slipped his hand over the small fingers curved around his arm and closing his eyes again, leaned his head back. *A fine idea indeed. I thank you.*

Chapter 14

The last hour felt like ten to Jun as she dismissed the men hired to add twenty more junks to her fleet. How was she expected to concentrate when Will was waiting for her? For the last twenty minutes alone, she secretly used the sign for *'please,'* as in please stop talking and stop showing me new hull designs and *please* let us be finished.

"Are you feeling unwell?" asked Peng. The pointed angle of his eyebrows met in a sharp frown.

Jun bit her lip to keep from screaming. "No, why do you ask?" *Please let me leave...*

"You've looked flushed all afternoon and keep touching your chest. Are you having pains? Should I fetch your physician?"

"I'm fine, truly. Nothing that a bit of peace cannot cure." She saw her chance to escape. "If you'll excuse me."

Please, no one call my name. She moved with a determined clip to her stride, but as she pushed through the doorway into her private quarters, Jun hesitated. She still didn't have a good answer to the question Will posed earlier.

The words he wrote had churned in her mind since she'd left him to wait for her. *'What are we doing?'*

"I don't know." She threw her hands wide and spoke to an empty room. Once Will kissed her, her mind hadn't been able to think of much else. Jun brushed her fingertips over her lips, savoring the memory. He needed to kiss her again, and soon.

The entire scene had been her idea, bringing him back to the exact moment they had been interrupted. But once there, Will took command as he had the night before, capturing her, plundering her mouth, stealing her breath. Jun smiled a small, seductive smile. Capturing, plundering, stealing… He might be a merchant captain, but he sure as hell kissed like a pirate—not that she'd been kissed by many.

Yes, he needed to kiss her again.

She pulled her armor off once more, reveling in the lightness. Was he still in the garden? Had he stayed? Jun headed toward the doors. In her haste to join him, she almost forgot to remove her headdress. Pulling it from her head, she tossed it aside, smoothed her hair, and hurried into the garden where she nearly collided with Ting.

Ting held up her hands to stop her. "Mistress, you must come see where my mischievous daughter chose to take her afternoon rest."

"Is Captain Quinn still here?" Jun loved Qi, but hoped she wasn't bothering Will.

"Yes, come see." Ting led the way before turning and laying a finger over her lips. "Shhh, I found them just this way." She swept her hand toward the alcove.

Jun's heart flooded at the sight of Will and Qi sitting side by side, with the child innocently curled around his arm, sleeping soundly against his chest. Will held Qi's tiny hand.

Jun made a sound like air leaving a set of bellows. In her brutal world of battles and bloody conquests, fleets of hardened, vicious men, when was the last time she had seen something so tender and dear? The sight touched a hidden maternal corner of her heart she didn't know she had. If she hadn't already had feelings for Will, she would have melted into his arms in that single moment.

"I should take her from him," Ting whispered, "but they looked so content. I didn't want to disturb them."

"No," Jun sighed softly as her heart ached at the sweetness of it. "Leave them."

"I have mistress's bath water warming. Shall I prepare it for you now? Bring your tea?"

"Aye…"

Ting hurried away on silent feet. Jun smiled as she returned to her rooms. A small envious part of her wishing she was the one resting against the strong wall of Will's chest. She hoped to change places with Qi soon.

Standing before a deep copper tub of milky soft water, Jun stepped out of her clothing, before testing the temperature and stepping into the luxurious bath.

The tepid water slipped like gentle waves over her skin, washing away the cold business of the day. Somehow today, everything felt different. As if her skin had become more sensitive, more receptive to the sensuous feel of things around her.

Taking the thick bar of rose soap, she ran the petal-laced bar slowly over her shoulder and down one arm. Soaping her leg next. Shivering as she trailed the lather high on her inner thigh.

Jun sighed with pleasure as she continued the soapy trail over her belly to suds the bow of her breasts. The jolt of pure longing as she ran the bar over her nipple made her gasp and she dropped the soap. Her free hand teased at the firm tip, fanning the flame of the fire that had started to build within her. The flicker of flame that had begun long before she climbed into this heavenly bath. In truth, this fire had ignited the first time she'd been captured by a pair of topaz eyes.

It was him. Will's touch that she craved. His mouth on hers. His hands on her body. Had she ever hungered for anything so much in her life?

Just the thought of it sent another tremor along her limbs. Jun slipped her hand lower, but when she reached the smooth apex of her thighs she stopped. A thin thread of fear wrapped around her heart.

Her tattoo. The ink that marked her as a whore. How would Will react when he saw it? She could imagine a look of disgust on his face. Would he even know what it meant, and if he did, would he give her the chance to explain? What if he didn't believe she'd only lain with Jian Fu?

The water in the bath had begun to turn cold. Her thoughts, however, had chilled more than the tub. She shivered and moved to pull herself from the water when she caught sight of the very man crowding her thoughts while shifting and whipping her emotions into a froth.

Will leaned against the framework of the door casually enjoying the view of her bathing. How long had he been there?

Jun crossed her arms over her chest and ducked back beneath the water, sloshing a great wave of it to the floor. Will's eyes followed the flood before returning his gaze to hers with a grin.

"You shouldn't be here. Ting? Where is Ting? Did you see me…? Why on earth am I talking?" Her heart raced faster than her words.

The way he watched her lips was so terribly seductive. She instinctively pressed them together to stop the flow, which only invited his gaze to travel lower. Jun could feel the heat of his gaze upon her skin. Searing a path across her collarbone, and down the slick pathway between her breasts to sizzle when it reached the soapy remains of her bath.

Her body tingled with desire "Oh…you really shouldn't be here…" she whispered.

Jun startled as he pushed away from the doorframe and moved toward her. He lifted a wide, plush drying cloth from a small pile next to the tub, unfolded it, and held it wide in invitation. When her gaze darted back to his, he raised a teasing eyebrow.

"No." She shook her head at him, before snatching at the towel. Jun ignored the expectant look upon his face and swirled a finger telling him to turn away.

A smile spread across his face as he followed her instruction. Jun started to rise, but a cheating peek over his shoulder stopped her once more.

"Do you want me to freeze to death in my own bath?" She twirled her finger once more. "If you keep sneaking glances at me, I'm not coming out."

Cautiously, she began to rise again. Ready at any second to dive for cover once more. She kept her eyes on him as she stepped out of the tub while wrapping herself in the drying cloth.

Jun reached for her robe and was quick to struggle into it with wet skin. "You can turn around now." She pulled the belt tight and touched his shoulder.

When he faced her once more, he did that slow scan of her body, sending heated messages straight to her core. Will ran a wide finger down the damp skin of her chest before hooking that finger behind the knot she'd tied in her belt and pulling her close for a kiss.

Unable to get over the fear that he'd pull her robe away from her body before she got a chance to explain her lotus, the kiss she gave him was quick and chaste. Jun pulled out of his grasp, his face, registering his confusion at her rather hasty rejection.

Shaking her head, frustration warred within her. Jun held up a hand. "No...not no, but wait... Look at you, you don't understand. I did say no, but not no, I don't want you. No...I need to tell you...before... Damn it. I can't stop every time I need to write out a blasted conversation on a bloody rock. This is impossible!" Jun covered her eyes with her hand.

When she lowered her hand, Will was walking away. Her stomach sank and she shivered at the chill. "Oh, no..."

She caught him as he moved through the doorway, circling a fist over her heart. '*Sorry, sorry, sorry.*' "I'm sorry. I wasn't yelling at you to stop. I was yelling at me. At the situation. I *want* you to kiss me, let you slip away my robe and touch me. Have you lift me in your arms and carry me to my bed. I *want* to be with you and make love to you. Spend an entire night *not* talking. It's just right this moment, I need to speak to you, and somehow make you understand."

Searching his face, Jun only saw the proud set of his jaw and the cool distance in his eyes. She cupped his cheek and lifted on her toes to kiss him. "I'm sorry." She said the words against his lips as she continued to sign the word.

Jun kissed him again before taking his hand and leading him into her bed chamber. She held up one finger, asking him to wait a moment, while she moved to her table and gathered paper and quill. She lifted it so he would see before she set to pouring out her story on the page.

She told him everything about her past. About Jian Fu and the painted whores. It filled one entire side of the piece of paper and half of another. The ink smudged in her haste and stained her fingers, but she kept writing.

Then she offered him the pages. Pushed them into his hands. After an agonizing hesitation, he started to read. He stopped only once to look at her, but she tapped on the sheet to keep him reading.

Will shifted the pages and continued. When he finished, he lifted his eyes to hers. She was too nervous to try and read his expression. Thankfully he couldn't hear her heart trying to beat its way through her ribs.

Jun took one step back and held tight to Will's gaze as she untied the belt at her waist, opened her robe, and let it fall to the floor. She stood with her arms pinned to her sides waiting for him to scan her body, but he didn't. He never moved. Did he not want to look?

His eyes never left hers.

Chapter 15

In two strides, Will had her in his arms. The pages she'd given him fluttered forgotten to the floor. Good God, had he ever seen anything more incredible in his life than Jun baring her body and her soul to him? He crushed her mouth to his, catching the sob that wrenched from her throat. Lifting her, he held her body tight to his. Her story touched his heart and made him appreciate the amazing woman he already knew her to be, but it made no difference to how he was coming to feel about her. In truth, it only served to solidify what his body had been trying to tell his heart all along. Did she for one minute imagine he would hold her past against her? His past was hardly pure. None of it mattered. She was his in this moment. That is what mattered. He ran his hand down the curve of her back and over the slight bow of her ass. Her skin was still moist from her bath. She smelled of roses, and he wanted her more than he had wanted any other woman he'd ever met.

Will tore his mouth away from her lips to kiss his way to her shoulder. Sucking gently at the sweet flesh. Dipping slightly, he wrapped one arm under her behind and lifted her off her feet then moved them both to her bed.

The room's sparse furnishings were modest and low to the ground, but the distance of the bed to the ground was not near as important as the distance from him to her. His skin to hers. A sliver of space greatly hindered by the presence of his own clothing, which took a scant two seconds to remove.

Unlike his chambers, the walls surrounding Jun while she slept were of stone not paper. Windows set high allowed enough light from the waning day to see her stretched out next to him. He drank in every inch of her.

Jun slipped an arm about his neck and pulled his mouth back to hers. As the kiss deepened, Will traced a line down the front of her throat with the pad of his thumb. He followed the path with his mouth.

The vision of her pale breasts hadn't been a dream. They were exactly as he remembered. Jun arched her back as he sucked one pearled nipple into his mouth. She pulled on his hair and clutched at his shoulder. God, her skin tasted so sweet. Will moved his attention to her other breast, teasing and circling the tip with his tongue.

Beneath him, Jun moved like the sea. Her body rising and writhing like the waves as she stroked his back and his arms, urging him lower. He outlined the shape of her navel before kissing her there and moved lower still.

In the fading light, Will laid his outstretched hand over the inked flower adorning her sex. Each of his fingers reaching the outlined point of each delicate petal. He traced the lines on her skin. Skimmed the smooth colors that fanned across her.

The stem of the lotus ended where the first gentle fold of her sex began. When he lowered his mouth to lay a kiss there, her body shuddered beneath his lips.

Rising on one arm, he lifted himself to look into her eyes. Jun's chest rose and fell in short pants. He touched the place over her heart before making the sign she already knew.

'You are beautiful.'

Jun covered her face with one hand, but it wasn't until her body gave a small jerk did he realize she cried. He pulled her hand away, cupping her cheek, catching her tears as they trailed across her temple.

No, no... It tore at his heart to think he'd hurt her. He kissed her again.

Jun calmed beneath him. She gave him a watery smile before signing, *'Thank you.'*

Her show of such emotion stunned Will. She did believe her past would make him reject her. That somehow her tattoo would turn him away. He wished he could explain to her how wrong she was. He would have to show her instead.

Will stroked his hand down her side as he kissed her again. Taking her hand, he let her feel how much he wanted her. When Jun grasped hold of his erection, all explanations ended. There was no miscommunication. He wanted her, and she wanted him. No words were needed. Nothing else mattered.

They made love long into the night. Will's only complaint was that he couldn't see her when darkness finally claimed the room. Luckily, he'd learned every inch of her, emblazoned the image of her beautiful body forever in his mind. Exhausted, they slept just as his problem with the darkness was dissolving into the dawn.

Will came awake with a start. He couldn't move his arm. Images of him being held down by the British troops when they arrested him for treason flashed through the fog of his brain. But then the British bastard rolled toward him and pressed a soft pair of warm breasts into his side and draped a satiny thigh over his hip. *Jun...*

Her hair tickled across his chest, and his heart nearly burst with joy. She was still here, in his arms. Still here. She'd stayed with him the entire night. Not rushed off like a thief after she'd taken what she wanted. A smile tugged at his lips. He wouldn't have to go searching for his pants either. Hell, he didn't care if he ever found his pants again.

Will caught her knee and raised her thigh a wee bit higher to press her satined skin along the hardened ridge of his erection.

Would this insatiable need for her ever stop? Jun stirred in his arms and rocked her damp sex gently against his hip. *Bloody hell, I hope not.*

Will kissed her forehead and tightened his hold on her. Jun kissed his chest, murmuring something against his skin before pushing her hair out of the way so she could scorch a line of soft kisses up the side of his neck. Her breath teased his ear until she lightly bit his earlobe. Was she trying to drive him crazy?

In one fluid movement, Jun straddled him and took him inside her. Air rushed from his lungs as liquid fire shot through his veins. He grabbed at her hips and rocked upward, moving with her, finding their accelerated rhythm.

In the light of day, she was even more glorious than he thought last night. As she rode him faster and harder, Jun arched her back. The tips of her hair danced across the tops of his thighs. And when he traced the stem of her lotus lower to tease the slick flesh there, it was as if her whole being blossomed like the dawn around him.

* * * *

Against both of their wishes to stay locked in her room and each other's arms for the remainder of the day, Will slipped out of Jun's quarters and took a roundabout route to return to his room. Smiling, he stepped past a sleeping man resting against the wall in a side hall who smelled strongly of pickled cabbage. He was taller than Will had imagined.

Will bent to retrieve the thread that "secured" his room. It was then he noticed two men exiting another sleeping chamber farther down the hall. The two were followed by two more, and two more after that. Wasn't it a might early in the day for a party? All the men headed away from him, so they never saw him. But when Will caught a flash of purple heading out of the room, he took no chances and ducked inside.

He waited, wondering which direction Peng was headed, and more importantly, what was he doing meeting with that many men in the early hours of dawn. Will couldn't shake the uneasy feeling that the man was up to something. Reading the way Peng moved and acted around Jun, it wasn't adding up in Will's mind. Jun trusted him, and yet, there was a distinct tension there. Will could see it clearly, but Jun had nothing but praise for her first mate.

He'd keep an extra eye on him. Just in case his instincts were right—they were always right.

After a few hours of much needed rest, Will gathered his things and headed back to the great hall. He was anxious to start writing down the stories of the *Scarlet Night*, but he was more anxious to see Jun again. The simple thought of seeing her filled his body with the warming sensation of want.

They agreed over a quick exchange of scribbled notes between kisses that they would be discreet with their building relationship, but that didn't mean he wouldn't take every opportunity to be in her presence, or find hidden opportunities to slip away and steal a few quiet moments with her.

Will pulled in a deep breath. He could still smell her on his skin, and yet, he wanted more. When had he ever reacted this way about a woman? He tugged the tails of his tunic lower. It might be more of a challenge to be discreet if he was constantly walking around with a wooden cock in his pants, but it was a price he was happy to pay. Will pulled at his shirt again. He'd be happy to pick up the proper sized clothing and blessed boots later that afternoon. He'd ordered a fine outfit from the tailor in the village with his newly won coins.

The day's business had begun by the time he reached the hall. Jun was in her place of honor looking every bit the queen. The evidence of their night together still showed in a lingering blush upon her cheeks. Her tempting mouth and pinked lips looked properly kissed. It took all his strength not to march straight over to her and kiss them again.

Peng hovered to her right. His eyes shifting from the business in front of Jun to various points around the room, but before Will could determine where Peng's attention was focused, a small, curly-haired child bumped against Will's side.

Qi grinned up at him and offered him a sticky, purple-stained handful of berries. She counted them on the table and left him half before scooping up the others and scooting away a hair's breadth ahead of her mother.

Ting planted her hands on her hips and called after the child. Qi wasn't listening and dashed behind one of the deeply carved panels scattered along the walls of the hall to hide.

The next time Will saw Qi, she was once more entering the hall from behind the dais. Had she gotten past him somehow? It was possible. She was small and quick as lightning, and the hall was busy today. Men and women moved about their business. One child could certainly come and go without notice. Qi garnered no attention from anyone, save her mother, who performed her duties with a quiet grace all the while keeping one watchful eye on her daughter. No small feat, that. The girl was like cool dark water, slipping silently past.

Will stretched his shoulders. He found it tiring to pay attention to all that was going on around him and keep a watchful eye on Peng. Especially when his eye kept traveling back to gaze at Jun. He was counting the hours until he could have her back in his arms again. How much longer before he could sweep his hands over the slight gentle curves of her body. Feel her respond to his touches. How her thighs trembled at her arousal. The primal roll of her hips as she took him inside her. Arch of her back. The look upon her face when she reached her release.

He shifted in his seat at the tightness in his trousers and tugged on his hems. Damn it all, he needed to get to the village.

Will tore his gaze away from Jun. Behind her Peng stood with a dark scowl setting his features. Will focused on Peng's hand as it clenched and released the pommel of his sword. An impatient gesture? A brooding hovered around the man until his attention was captured by the arrival of a small contingent. Will recognized two of them. They were the same men he had seen that morning.

Peng's chin raised a fraction of an inch in acknowledgement of their arrival. Sliding Jun a side glance, he backed away from her without notice and slithered off the dais. Had he gone directly toward the group, Will would have ignored his growing suspicion, but the man feigned nonchalance while masking his movements through the room. All the while sending covert signals to the waiting men and furtive glances back at Jun.

It was after the group left and Will watched Peng from his vantage point, when all Will's warning flags began to fly. Peng waited. Almost counting the minutes before he could slip away. Was he meeting the men outside? Peng's gaze swept the room once more. Will lowered his head to disguise his gaze behind the ropes of his hair, but he never averted his eyes. Peng paid him no notice. Giving Jun a cursory glare, Peng darted from the great hall in a purple flash.

Perhaps now was the perfect time to head off to the village. Kill two birds...or one bird, one purple weasel.

Chapter 16

"General Peng, the crew of this ship has grown too large. We will do better to transfer half these men over to Commander—" Jun realized she was talking to herself. Peng was nowhere to be seen. He was just here. She scanned the hall. When had he slipped by her?

She frowned. Will was gone as well. Nothing remained from where he'd been sitting but a borrowed bottle of ink and what appeared to be a handful of berries. Where had he disappeared to and why did she have a sneaking suspicion the two vanishing men had something to do with one another?

Jun didn't see either man for the remainder of the day, and she'd grown tired of being distracted from her work whenever someone entered the hall eagerly hoping it was Will returning. It was bad enough getting through the day interrupted by constant thoughts of her night with Will. Reliving every moment, every touch, the pure magic of being with him.

Last evening had been beyond anything she could have imagined. Part of her felt disloyal comparing Will to Fu, but the truth was Fu was a selfish lover. It had always been her place to please him. She had been trained for it. Even though he rejected some of that training, he expected her to behave as a wife should and follow his wishes. Jun never initiated their lovemaking, but always came to him willingly when he wanted to lie with her. Their joining, however, had never inspired the passion she experienced with Will last night.

She barely recognized the woman she'd become in his arms. The play of his mouth and his touch both satisfied and tempted. As if each caress soothed and tortured at the same time until her body seemed to burst into a million stars.

And when she positioned herself atop, straddling him, taking control of his as well as her pleasure, she had unleashed something within herself.

All at once she was powerful in a way she'd never known power before, using her body to push them faster, stronger, driving each of them to an amazing climax.

Jun pulled her swollen lip between her teeth and shifted in her seat. Even now, her body hungered for him. Craved to feel him fill her. Touch the deepest part of her. Jun trembled with want. The tender ache of her sex pulsed for more.

Where was he?

It wasn't until she was finished for the day and retreated to the sanctuary of her rooms and garden that she found him again. Seeing him brought another fevered flush of heat to her skin and a renewed rush of wetness to her sex. Had she ever seen such a beautiful man?

Gone were his traditional Chinese clothes, which, in truth, hadn't suited him at all. In their place, he wore the more western style of trousers. They hugged the strength of his thighs in a rich cinnamon brown and tucked into beautiful high-polished black boots. A long, woven shirt of raw cream-colored silk fell over the contours of his shoulders and opened invitingly at the neck. Its full cut to accommodate the breadth of his shoulders was caught with a wide sash the color of dark wine to emphasize the taper of his waist. An open leather vest stained the rich hue of burnished copper completed him.

The sight took her breath.

If that wasn't enough to set her heart skipping about the confines of her chest, he was posed on one knee seemingly teaching Qi how to use a wooden spooled top. To Jun's amazement, it appeared he was being successful.

He showed her how to wrap a length of jute around the teardrop shape of the top before pulling sharply to set the top spinning. Qi was delighted and scrambled to catch the toy before mimicking Will and attempting to spin the top herself.

When Will saw Jun, he rose, leaving Qi to continue practicing. Closing the distance between them in one determined stride, he tipped Jun's chin with the tip of his finger and covered her lips with his before coaxing open her mouth with a sweep of his tongue. He was like a sensual wave, washing over her, surrounding her, carrying her away.

Qi stomped her feet behind him. Jun broke the kiss and peered around Will to find the child grinning at them.

"So much for being discreet." Jun pointed to Qi. "We're lucky she talks almost as much as you," she teased while stroking his cheek. Jun ran a hand over his new clothing, and made the only sign that was even close to the word she wanted. "You're beautiful...if only I knew the gesture for devastatingly handsome."

Qi's top skittered across the floor and Jun stepped away from Will to hand it back to her as Ting entered the garden bringing Jun's evening tea. Her cheeks brightened when she looked at Will. Setting the tray down, she bowed. Woven into the dark length of her hair was a pale-yellow ribbon.

"Shall I help you change, Mistress, before your tea?"

"Yes, please." Jun stroked the long sweep of Ting's hair. "You look lovely."

Ting tugged on the tail of the ribbon and flushed a brighter shade of pink. "Captain Quinn has given us many gifts today. Sweets for your tea, toy for Qi, a ribbon… He is a most generous man."

"I agree." Jun watched as Will stooped to set the top spinning again.

Moving into Jun's private rooms, Ting worried. "Is it right that we accepted his gifts before you could approve?"

Jun slipped out of her rigid attire. "Captain Quinn's actions do not fall under my command. What he chooses to do is his own. I'm happy he's been so kind to you and Qi."

"Have you seen how she works her top?" Ting poured warm water from a tall silver ewer. "He shows her such patience." She helped Jun with her ties and confided. "He has brought something else for you as well."

"Other than sweets for my tea?" Ting nodded with a wide smile. A gift? For her? A tickle of childish excitement rushed through her. When was the last time she received any kind of gift? Fu was not given to lavish her with trinkets or ornaments. Her family had been too poor to know such indulgence.

"I have been so curious to see what it is." Ting handed her a fat sea sponge.

Jun lathered the sponge and began wiping the grime of the day from her skin. "I'm curious myself."

Ting gathered Jun's discarded garments. "Perhaps he wishes to give it to you when you are alone. He has a great fondness for you, I think. I'll be quick to finish here and take Qi away."

"Let her play. Whatever my gift, I'm sure it can wait." Jun said, even as her inquisitive nature nibbled at her.

A short time later, Jun sipped at a cup of tepid tea as Ting gathered Qi for the evening. The child wasn't as eager to leave, however, and wound herself around Will's lower leg. But Will shook his head, tapped his chin and with a stern point of his finger Qi heaved a dramatic sigh and went away with her mother.

Jun wrote on the slate tablet, *You are very good with her. She has never responded to anyone like she has with you.*

Will took the slate from her fingers. *There is more to her than you believe.*

Jun read his words with a frown and Will responded by wiping the stone clean and continuing. *She's not simple. Very smart.*

Jun was quick to add a note below his words. *She doesn't even speak.* As soon as she had written the words she tried to erase them before he could read them as if she were implying that somehow by the same logic, Will was simple as well. A shadow passed over his eyes. She'd insulted him. Jun shook her head. "That isn't what I meant." She signed *'Sorry.'*

Will pulled back the stone. *She counts. Knows that half of ten is five. Has made secret passageways for herself throughout the palace. Follows instructions easily. Quick to learn.* He wrote so quickly, Jun reached for his hand as he wrote, *Qi can't hear.*

The air left her lungs in a rush as Jun stared at his words. He erased them and wrote, *Not totally deaf. She may hear some sounds, but I see the signs. Are you sure?*

Will nodded. *I was like her. Needs a way to communicate. Already taught her some words. Come. Go. Mother. Good. Bad. Yes. No. My name is Qi. I want more berries.* As Will wrote them on the stone, he made the simple gestures. *There are books she needs.*

"So we can help her." Jun whispered in awe. She slipped her hand over his and gave it a squeeze. "I wouldn't have guessed, but now that you say it, I see where you may be right. Many will still believe she is cursed for her mixed heritage, but if she cannot hear… I'll see to it she gets the books and tutors she needs. Help Ting understand."

Will studied her mouth. It was as if he touched her with his gaze. He may have saved that sweet child from a life of silent despair. Her heart filled to overflowing. He may have saved her from a similar fate, as well. Had anyone ever made her feel this much joy?

Setting her cup aside, she leaned over to Will and kissed him. *'Thank you.'*

The kiss deepened. Will slipped his hand behind her neck and held her to him. Stroking a lazy pathway down the front of her throat and back again with his thumb.

Will eased away. His gaze roaming over each of her features as if he were trying to commit them all to memory. After dropping another quick kiss onto her mouth, he stood and moved into a shadowy corner of the garden where he retrieved a long parcel wrapped in coarse cloth and tied with a length of hemp.

Excitement flared in her as he placed it in her lap. Jun pointed to her chest coyly asking if it was indeed for her. Will smiled his beautiful smile as she tugged at the twine.

Unwrapping the gift, tears filled Jun's eyes. In her arms, she held a stunning pipa. The neck of the instrument swept into a gentle arc like the squared hull of a junk, carved with roses and vines tinted in deep reds and greens with sweeping touches of gold. Below, four onyx tuning pegs were inlaid with bands of golden filigree. The carvings and rich painting continued along the fingerboard and swept into the rounded base. Rich glossed wood bowed the back of the pipa with a thin tendril of gold gracing the center spine.

"Where did you find such a magnificent instrument?" Jun reverently traced the fragile gilt-tipped petals of a rose.

Will lifted the neck of the pipa and put it to her shoulder before placing her hand on its strings. He wanted her to play.

Blinking back tears of gratitude, she plucked a few strings and adjusted the tuning pegs. Jun played a gentle tune for him. One she played often. A soft song that spoke of a maiden's loss of her true love. Her fingers moved over the silken strings. Will crouched before her and slipped his hands to rest on the instrument's bellied base. "Listening" to the music with his fingertips. Feeling the instruments vibration.

A look of pure wonder crossed Will's features as he followed the movement of her fingers. His smile spread across his handsome face… and squeezed at her heart. Jun kept playing as her tears fell unchecked and realization caught her breath.

She loved this man.

Her fingers stumbled over the chords. *She loved him.* Her heart nearly burst with the intensity of it.

When she stopped playing, Will's eyes flew to hers. Seeing her tears, he was quick to set the pipa aside and pulled her into his arms. He crushed her to his chest and rained kisses over her cheeks before taking her mouth with his.

Jun clung to him, grabbing a handful of his thick hair; she parted her lips to the imploring sweep of his tongue. She responded with a ravenous kiss of her own. Their heated breaths danced as their kisses became more demanding.

Will's hold tightened to press her to him. The long, hard ridge of his arousal constrained between them. His obvious want of her needed no words.

Jun's head spun. Her body shuddered with need. This was senseless. Wonderfully, ridiculously irrational. Yes, he was handsome and strong, but he was a total stranger. An unexpected gift cast at her feet from the sea. He had also shown himself to be caring and devoted to his lost crew, and the kindness he showed to Qi and to her…

And in her bed, he'd shown her a passion she had yet to discover. Her body responded to his as if she was finally breaking the surface of a dark sea. Jun was lost. Swept away. Hopelessly and completely. She was in love.

Will shifted his hold and rose with her in his arms. Her body lay flush against his. Tight to him. Their mouths hungering for one another as he carried her into a shadowed corner of the garden.

Amongst the vivid blossoms under the darkening sky, they lay together on thick cushions. Jun fought her impatience and removed each piece of his clothing with gentle care as if she were unwrapping yet another gift. Playing his muscles like the silken strings of her lute. Strumming her fingers over the satin texture of his skin. Jun's being sang as they came together in the unrushed, quiet music that only lovers know.

And when it was over, when they lay spent, entangled arms and legs, each struggling to catch their breaths, Jun breathed against his warm, damp skin.

"I...I love you."

Will lifted his head to look into her face. He ran his fingertips over her mouth with a frown. He hadn't heard her, of course. Had it been easier for her to say those three words knowing full well he couldn't hear them? Jun gave a tiny shake of her head before kissing his fingertips and guiding his arm around her. She rested her cheek against his wide chest.

With her ear to Will's chest, she could hear the strong beat of his heart. His lungs pulled in deep steady breaths. Her sex still shimmered with tiny tremors, and the only thing she could think of was that Will would never hear her tell him she loved him. Could she have uttered the words otherwise not knowing if he shared her feelings? She knew the answer to that. Jun closed her eyes tight. When had she become such a coward?

Drawing her sword and fighting for her life was one thing. Opening up her heart to a man, any man, was far more dangerous. Jun risked her life every day. Fought to stay at the top of her pirate kingdom. Sailing into battle was part of who she was. It was her life.

But to risk her heart... Her belly tightened at the thought. That would mean jeopardizing more than her life and her empire; it would be endangering her soul.

Chapter 17

Jun lay in the warmth of Will's embrace for a long time, listening to the gentle breathing of his sleep, while she wrestled with the reality of what was happening between them. Yes, she loved him, but he was still so much a stranger to her. An odd thing to think when you're lying naked with a man, your body still craving his, but it was the truth. Was that part of his allure? His mysterious appeal?

She closed her eyes and tried to find her own sleep, but her thoughts kept churning in her mind. There was a reason she hadn't been close to a man in the years since Fu's death. Relationships complicated things, and a future with a man like Will was riddled with complications beyond the fact that she was a bloody pirate trying to rule a legion of cutthroat outlaws. She was a criminal. Whole countries wanted her head on a spike. Such a life was no place for dreams of love and life and happily ever after.

Even if her life wasn't full of violence and peril, there was little hope for them. Will was a westerner. Her culture alone forbade any union between them. If she defied convention and continued to be with him…and a child was conceived? While she and Fu used every precaution to assure no children would be a result of their union, a tiny, idealist part of Jun still hoped that one day she would be a mother. But if a child were conceived, it would be shunned by her own people. Like Qi.

Watching Ting and Qi together was bittersweet for her, because until lately, Jun hadn't even considered the possibility of holding her own child in her arms. But to subject a child to the life of an outcast…quite possibly a deaf child.

In her mind, she could still see Will teaching Qi to spin her top. Recognizing her hearing problem, teaching Qi her first words. He would make a fine father to some lucky babe. Of course, in Jun's mind, he would have a son first.

Jun sat up and shook her head. She had to get these ridiculous thoughts out of her head, but when she looked down at Will's sleeping form, she disregarded all her objections and concerns and could almost picture their sweet baby. He would be beautiful. Smart, strong. A perfect son with his father's insightful, soulful topaz eyes.

Stop it! Jun rose and stepped away from Will to find her robe. After donning it, she covered Will with as much as his shirt would cover and moved away from him.

Back at the small table in the alcove, Jun finished her cold tea and nibbled a tender bit of sweet honey cake. Another of Will's gifts. He'd shown them such kindness. Her new pipa was stunning. She didn't dare touch it with her honeyed fingers, but knew she would treasure it always. And she would never forget the look on his face when she played. As improbable as it all was, Jun's heart refused to let her give up on the idea that perhaps Will shared some of her feelings as well.

It was then Jun noticed Will's book resting next to the opposite cushion. Giving a quick peek down the garden path, she reached around the table and picked it up. The burnished silver latch was unlocked and yet, she hesitated opening the fine leather-bound logbook. Jun traced the detailed corner caps. She'd meant to ask him about looking at it, but her intentions had gotten lost somewhere between Qi and gifts and kisses that continued to rob her of rational thought and sear her from the inside out.

Jun gave another glance down the path. A small glimpse wouldn't do any harm. She raised the wick on a nearby lantern.

Cradling the log, it fell open to midway through the pages where the place was marked by a small square of red sail cloth. Jun recognized it at once. The rough edges had been neatly trimmed, but it was the bit of sail Will had retrieved from the wreckage on the beach.

Jun fingered the cloth's rich color and tried to picture Will's ship. She'd forgotten its name. Didn't know what type of ship it was, but could imagine it with its fine red sails bowed, riding the tips of the waves. Jun could imagine him, too, standing at the helm. Legs astride. The spray of the water. The bite of the wind. Sunlight gleaming off his dark skin. He would have made a striking pose.

She set the scrap of sail in her lap and lifted the book closer. His handwriting was a bit difficult to decipher in ink. Jun raised the wick of the lantern once again and read:

I became a member of the Scarlet Night *crew sometime between the ages of four and five. Having no knowledge of the day of my birth, this is as good a guess as I can make. Pulled from the gutters of Port Royal, Jamaica, I made my mark to the Ship's Articles and began my life as a privateer in the year 1685 as a cabin boy.*

Jun's eyes shot up the path. *Of course…I knew he had to be more than a simple merchant seaman. Bloody hell…He's a pirate.* Somehow that bit of information made him even more attractive. And impressive. A deaf merchant was one thing, but a pirate who couldn't hear? How had he survived a life filled with battles and raids, not to mention two score years of storms and living a life at sea? It certainly explained the scars on his back, as well.

She kept reading:

My first weeks were hellish. Seasick and unfamiliar with life aboard ship, I was always where I shouldn't be at all the worst times. After a swinging block nearly cleaved my skull in two, and a whipping rope flayed open my forehead, they gave me the nickname of Bump. A name that would follow me through most of my life. Few knew my given name of William, and not even I knew of my surname. Quinn was gifted to me by the woman who helped raise me and kept me alive for more years than I deserved. Alice Tupper Quinn, known to the crew of the Scarlet Night *as Tupper.*

Jun continued to read Will's accounts of Tupper and her husband Captain Gavin Quinn. How they battled the vile slave trade flowing from the African coast and fought side by side until… *that horrible day. June 7, 1692 when the sea rose up and swallowed the earth.*

Will recounted in gruesome detail the great earthquake that hit the island of Jamaica on that morning. He'd felt the tremors. Had some intuitive warning of what was to come, but couldn't make anyone understand what he was sensing. Then it was too late. Will stood in the aft of the ship and watched a great blood red cloud rise above the city of Port Royal as the ground seemed to dissolve before his eyes. He witnessed buildings sinking. Ships being dragged down by their anchors. People on the beach…he'd seen them scratching for the sky before the waters rushed from the land only to return with a great wave of vengeance. It wiped part of the world away and erased all the life that had been there. He'd seen it all.

His words were so raw and poignant. Jun could picture everything. It broke her heart. Will had been a young boy when he'd lost Gavin Quinn in the earthquake, by his accounts they'd lost most of their crew as well that day. What touched her most was his sense of guilt. That somehow, he could have saved them. Warned them in time. He still carried that burden of regret and responsibility to this day for something that was completely beyond his control.

Jun cradled the book to her chest. There was more to read. He was telling the story of his life. Part of her felt strange, peering into his personal writings, but it explained so much. Now she understood the depth of his anguish over losing his ship and his crew. They were more than that. He'd lost his family. His home. First the man who held the place of his father all those years ago, and now his "mother." And the weight of being the one in command of the *Scarlet Night* when the ship was lost? To a man who held duty and responsibility to such a high degree. No wonder he'd been so devastated.

And it was also no wonder he was so concerned with the teaching of a small child. He was trying to save Qi as Gavin and Tupper Quinn had once saved him. Given him a life, even one amongst thieves and villains. They taught him how to survive the challenges he faced. How to fight in battle and live another day. But more than all that, they taught him about honor, duty, and love.

Jun's heart swelled. Had she not already been completely captivated by him, these revelations would have led her there. William "Bump" Quinn was a good man. And a fierce bloody pirate to boot!

At the crunch of shells in the walk, Jun startled and rushed to return Will's book to where it had sat. Her heart pounded at the threat of being caught prying into his personal writings.

Coming out of the shadows, the sight of him reaffirmed all she was feeling for him. He'd slipped his pants back on, but carried the rest of his belongings over one arm. Jun drank in the seductive sight of him. The span of his chest and the way the lantern light shone on his beautiful skin as it rode the play of muscles beneath.

He'd been in a hurry to find her. She could tell because he'd forgotten to button the top two buttons on his fitted trousers allowing them to ride below his waist. Offering her a tempting view of that ridge of muscle riding over his hip. The effect was devastating. How had she ever mistaken him for a simple merchant? If any man looked and strode with the confidence of a pirate, it was Will.

Her fingers curled in a desire to touch him as Jun realized she still held the bit of red sail in her lap. She scrambled to her feet and shoved it into her pocket. How could she get it back into the book without him catching her?

Jun smiled hoping to disguise her rush of guilt from shining like a beacon on her face. One hand held firmly around the evidence in her pocket while the other pressed at the sudden flock of birds trying to flap their way out of her stomach.

When Will reached her, he returned her smile before dropping his things on top of his book. Her heart followed the drop of his clothing. How would she return the bit of sail now?

He lifted a bit of honey cake and popped the morsel into his mouth. A second piece he fed to her, then licked the sweetness from his fingers as he watched her mouth work. Between the warm smell of his skin so close, and the seductive way he looked at her, parts of her anatomy began melting faster than the honey on her tongue.

Her body trembled with her insatiable need of him. To hell with the guilty evidence held in her pocket. She'd figure out how to return it later.

Then Will made the small gesture of tapping his fingertips together. Jun searched through the sensual fog clouding her brain. Wasn't that one of the signs he had taught Qi? It took her a moment to remember.

'More.' He was asking if she wanted more.

Oh, yes, please. She clumsily signed, *'Yes, I want more.'*

His pleasure at her signing was obvious, but when he reached for more cake, she laid a gentle hand on his arm and made the sign for *'No.'* She pushed the cake away and guided his hand to cradle her cheek.

'More.' She made the sign then tapped her lips. Will gave her a smoldering stare as the corner of his mouth lifted before he dropped a single chaste kiss upon her lips. *'More.'* She ran her palms over the muscles of his chest and stopped to tease the flat disks of his nipples with a sweep of her thumbs.

Will pulled in a great breath swelling his chest beneath her touch. The tips of his nipples hardened under her strokes. His eyes drifted closed. Fine goose bumps disturbed the smoothness of his skin.

When he opened his eyes, he made another series of signs. Most of which Jun had never seen before, until he got to the last. She recognized the sign for want. It was almost a desperate grasping gesture. Was he telling her he wanted her, or asking if she wanted him?

Jun skipped her fingertips over the ridges of his abdomen before hooking one into the open waistband of his trousers. She watched his throat work. When she brushed the tip of his erection, his lips parted with a small gasp. He stood perfectly still.

Leaning forward she whispered against his lips. "Yes, I want. I want all of you." She slipped another of his buttons from its home. She smiled at the obvious effect she was having on Will. It was her turn to make him tremble. Sliding her fingers lower she grasped the full width of him. "Seems I can't get enough…"

With her free hand, she guided Will's touch to her breast before kissing him again. All the while, she played in long slow strokes over the firmness of his cock.

Will kneaded her breast in the same slow torturous fashion. His body practically hummed with steeled restraint. He was holding back. Letting her be the seducer. Giving her the lead, giving himself over to her, and she was reveling in the sense of power it gave her.

He pulsed in her hand. It was Jun's turn to gasp as a damp rush to her own sex echoed his desire. She bit his lip gently before pulling away. Now, she wanted him now. They both were breathless with need.

Jun took Will's hand from her breast and tugged him toward her bed chamber. As he headed in that direction, Jun was quick to slip behind him. At his questioning glance, she pointed to the lantern that still burned high. She snuffed out the light, and in one covert rush stuffed the square of red sail back between the pages of his book. Where it fell, she didn't care. All that mattered was she was back leading him to her bed before his eyes could adjust to the darkness.

Inside she lit a single candle casting gentle shadows throughout the room. As in the garden, Will held himself in check allowing Jun to play the seducer. The muscle in his jaw told her just how restrained he was being when she took her time stripping him of his only article of clothing.

Buttons slipped from their holes, one after the next, exposed him. Jun moved closer, pressing her chest to his as she slid her hands over his hips and under his waistband to skim his trousers off the curve of his taut backside and push them lower.

Will's breath fluttered the hair at her temples. When she lifted her gaze to his, the intensity of his stare ratcheted her own breathing. Dropping her chin, she gave him her most seductive smile and tugged at the ties of her robe. Instead of the garment joining his trousers in a cascading liquid puddle of silk at their feet, the belt knotted and held fast.

Jun bit her lip and tried again with the same result. She groaned in frustration and dropped her gaze to the stubborn tangle. "Damn it. You touch it and it practically dissolves. I try and it locks so tight, I'll have to find a dirk to cut the bloody thing off me." Her fingers plucked at the disobedient silk.

Will stilled her hands, and captured her gaze again. She shook her head and held her hands to her sides in surrender. "You can try, but a blade may be the only—"

The robe slipped to the floor.

"How…?" She lifted her eyebrows in surprise. Will tipped one corner of his mouth as he lifted his hand and blew on his fingertips as if they were hot.

Jun threw back her head and laughed before winding her arms around his neck. "I'll never doubt your magic fingers again." She stood on tip toes to kiss him as she backed them toward the bed and pulled Will down atop her.

Spreading her legs, she offered herself up to him and he took her in one fiery thrust. Jun cried out in pleasure as she gripped at his shoulders. Will braced himself above her and pushed into her again. The ends of his hair tickled her chest.

Jun gasped at the strength of his thrusts. Raising her hips to the building pleasure, she released her hold upon his arms to tap her fingertips together... *'More... More... More....'*

Chapter 18

Will was alone when he rose the following morning. The sun was just lightening the sky. He hadn't slept long, but he was surprisingly refreshed. Perhaps the adrenaline from the late hours of last night was still pumping through his veins.

After Jun had fallen into a sated sleep lying across his chest, he had lain awake, relishing the weight of her body on his. Comforted by her warmth while he tried to sort out the clutter of his thoughts.

Unlike the silk tie of her robe, his mind wouldn't untangle so easily. He was in love with her. If there was one certainty in all of this, that was it. What good that realization would be, was another story.

He was still a captain without a ship. A pirate without a crew and a price on his head. Other than the clothes on his back, a second-hand pistol, and a handful of coins, he had nothing to offer. His future continued to be one vast, empty ocean with nothing to navigate her by. How could he pledge his love and life to a woman like Jian Jun when her wealth and empire encompassed the entire South China Sea, and his barely filled a pocket?

But last night… he gave her something he'd never given another woman. He'd made love to her with his whole heart. Body and soul. Gave her everything he was beyond ego. Beyond roles. He'd poured all the love he felt for her into their joining, and it had never been so good.

Now all he had to do was figure out how to stay in her life and keep her in his.

Slipping on his trousers, he went in search of her. The garden was empty. Ting and Qi had yet to arrive for the day. Cold tea and stale cake still sat on the small table in the alcove. Had Jun been called away?

He dressed. Slid his feet into his new boots. The stiff leather pinched at his heel. It would take him weeks to break them in. He donned his vest and left his baldric to one side. A bit of red caught his attention. Out of the end of his log book, the bit of sail he'd kept from the *Scarlet Night* peeked out between the pages.

Will lifted the book. The sailcloth wasn't where he had left it, and the only one who could have moved it would have been Jun. Had she read the log? She must have done so while he slept in the garden. His clothes hadn't moved from where he dropped them, so she must have looked at it before then.

That would explain the wide-eyed smile she gave him when he rejoined her last night. She'd been afraid to be caught. How long had he been asleep and more important, how much had she read? Was her seduction last night nothing more than a clever distraction? No, he couldn't bring himself to believe that.

He fingered the cloth and frowned. She had never pressed him on the details of his past, perhaps because she already knew the truth and it was of no consequence to her. Then why not tell him? The same could be asked of him, however. Fear of her knowing the British had a price on his head was what kept him silent all this time. But if she discovered it on her own, she wasn't showing any signs of anger that he'd kept the truth from her.

Maybe he was wrong. Could be the book fell and she simply picked it up. If anything, he felt a deeper connection after he found her here last night. Yes, she was a powerful, influential woman, but guile and manipulation did not describe her. She could not have faked what happened between them in her bed. He would have seen it. Sensed it. He was too good at reading people to be blind as well as deaf.

Will flipped through the pages of the log. He was wrong to jump to conclusions, but it did strengthen his resolve. He'd give her the book tonight, and let her read the truth. If he was ever to figure out a way to be with her in the future, he wanted her to know the whole story about who he was.

He ran his thumb over the edges of the pages as he wondered what Jun's reaction would be to his truth. It was then he noticed several gaps when he fanned the pages. He opened the book wide. *Son of a bitch...*

Pages were missing in several places. A half dozen in total. And they had been meticulously, almost invisibly removed, not haphazardly torn from the binding. Someone used a blade to extract them. Will scanned the neighboring pages. What was taken were entries dated back to when the *Scarlet Night* battled around the Cape of Good Hope. It was his accounting of the discovery of the deep inner channel close to the shore which kept the *Night* from bearing the worst of the conditions found there.

Certainly, that would be useful if you wanted to find a quicker way into the Atlantic. An unease crept up his spine. If someone wanted to extend the reach of their enormous fleet and set about engaging more ships, amassing more wealth, that would be a tidy bit of information, indeed. And there was only one *someone* who he'd been foolish enough to let down his guard.

It couldn't have been Jun, but who else? All this time he'd been wary and watchful of Peng, but perhaps it had been Jun all along. And like a fool, he'd fallen for her and let her lead him around by the cock. Had she set out to seduce him all along, or had she actually developed some feelings for him?

Anger warred with blinding hurt. He couldn't be wrong about her. About them. Could he? She couldn't be so conniving. No, he wouldn't believe it.

He reached for his baldric. There was only one way to know for sure.

By the time his boot hit the tiled floor of the grand hall, Will had convinced himself that there had to be another explanation.

It was still early. The hall was near empty when he arrived. Jun and Peng were talking on the dais.

They both noticed him at the same time. Will's attention honed in on the tiniest detail of Jun's posture. Her easy smile faded as quickly as it came, seconds before he was ambushed from behind by several men. They leapt on his back and dragged him to the floor.

He fought off one and reached for his pistol, only to have his arm caught and hauled behind his back. Rolling, he rammed his head against another's face and felt the man's nose snap. Will kicked off another while the two on his right side tried to wrench his arm from his shoulder, pulling it behind him. His weapons seized.

A fist hit him from the left, knocking him down again. Lights exploded in his head. When the cold circle of a gun barrel jammed into his temple, he stopped fighting. One of the men planted his knee in the center of Will's back pinning him to the floor, threatening to snap him in half before his left arm suffered the same fate as his right.

God, they were tying his hands! A familiar panic iced through his veins, but the pistol pointed at his head forced him to choke down his fear. Will twisted his head. He could see Jun. Peng stood between them, keeping her from him. Seemingly protecting her from Will. He needed his hands to speak. What the hell were they doing? He wouldn't hurt her; he needed to speak to her. *Jun!*

Will bucked at his restraints until something heavy and solid cracked the back of his skull.

* * * *

"What the hell are you doing? Let him go!" Jun watched in horror as Peng's men seized Will and brought him to the floor.

Peng stepped in front of her and held her by her shoulders. "The man is a spy."

"That's impossible, let me pass." Jun attempted to side step him, but he continued to block her way. "Release him."

"He is a serious threat to you, Jun. Trust me in this. I've ordered him removed at once."

"You've ordered?" Peng continued blocking her from going to Will. "Get your hands off me or lose them. I know nothing of any threat, from Captain Quinn. What are you talking about? What proof do you have?"

"You remember, I sent a query through the fleet. Information arrived at first light. The last known reports of a ship known as the *Scarlet Night* came from one of our very own men. The *Scarlet Night* was captured more than two years ago by the British Navy and all hands were arrested and charged with treason. They were sentenced to hang." Peng looked back at his men. "I believe the British sent this man to spy on us. He's lied to us both. Our man also reported that he sailed on the *Night* for several years. He knew Captain Quinn. Two of them. Neither one of them were named William. There is no such man. The British sent him to spy on us. He's part of a clever plot to infiltrate our empire."

"That's ridiculous. If you'll get out of my way..." Jun gasped as she watched Will knocked unconscious. "Damn it, Peng. I read his journal. What you're saying is wrong."

"Have you been so blinded by your obvious feelings for the man that you believe something he's scribbled on a page? In a book he just so happened to leave out for you to find? You're too clever to fall for such a simple hoax."

Jun shook him off. "You don't know what you're talking about."

"I think I do." He stared her down. Behind him, his men dragged Will from the hall. "Forget your pride and consider for one moment that our information is right. His presence is a severe threat to you and all you've fought so hard to achieve. The British have launched a dozen campaigns to end our command of these waters together with the Chinese. They would stop at nothing to cut off the head of the Dragon, dismantle the fleet, and extinguish our fire."

A sharp claw of poisonous doubt scratched a bitter path down her spine. "You're wrong about Will. If there is such a plot against us, I can't believe he's a part of it."

Peng gave her a pitying look. "You're letting your feelings cloud what you know to be true."

Damn him. Jun couldn't think past the fact that she may have lost her heart to a man who was plotting to kill her. No! What was she thinking? She wasn't an idiot. She hadn't gotten to where she was by being weak and foolish.

Jun crossed her arms over her chest. She trusted Will, and more importantly, she trusted her judgment. Peng was mistaken. She would get to the truth. "Who is the man who brings this information? I want to speak to him myself."

"I don't have his name. I'm not even sure which crew the information came from. It was passed from commander to commander. All I know is he, too, is a westerner. He has no reason to lie about his connection to the *Scarlet Night*. He signed an oath to you when he joined with us. What reason would he have to lie?" Peng looked over his shoulder with a pompous grin. "Opposed to the host of reasons for our unwanted guest to deceive us."

Jun narrowed her eyes and glared at Peng. "Track him down. I don't care how long it takes. I want to know who he is and if his information is first-hand or hearsay."

"Track him down?" Peng threw wide his hands and gaped at her as if she had lost her mind. "We have over nine hundred ships."

Hurt and anger flared in Jun, but at her core, it was fear nibbling its way through her belly. She needed answers and she needed them now. "I don't care if there are nine thousand. I want facts. Proof. Bring everything you can find to me at once."

Peng shook his head sadly. "I will do my best, but…"

"No excuses." Jun left the dais and moved to the place where the men had taken Will. His logbook had been trampled in the struggle. When she bent to pick it up, she noticed the smear of blood on the tiled floor. She straightened and turned back to Peng.

The muscle in Jun's jaw pulsed as the edges of her heart began to frost. "If your information is right, I will take Captain Quinn's head myself." Peng's pompous grin returned. "However, if you are wrong… it will be your blood that stains the blade of my sword."

Chapter 19

Jun rushed back to her private quarters and into the gardens before falling to her knees and losing the contents of her stomach. Ting rushed to her side and held her while she continued to wretch. Tears blurred her vision. This wasn't happening. Will couldn't have deceived her. The way he held her last night... They had made love for hours. He'd done everything she asked...and '*more.*'

She covered her eyes with a trembling hand. There had been a certain coolness to him when they stood in the garden, however. Jun's stomach recoiled as she remembered the restraint on his part. She believed he was letting her be the seductress. What if he... The whores of the Painted Palace had once lectured her on the dangers of getting emotionally attached. They taught her how to be cool...distant.

She heaved again. Ting wrestled the baldrics from her and loosened the hold of her armor. Jun moaned. Had she fallen in love with a man who'd been sent to snake his way into her bed? A ruse to penetrate her private space searching for any weakness in her empire? Give her enemies some vulnerability they could exploit? Had she been so desperate to be touched, so hungry for love that she ran blindly into Will's arms? It wasn't as if he forced himself upon her. She had been the aggressor. Jun gripped at her twisting stomach. She had reveled in her power to seduce him. Had she played into his hands? How could she have been so reckless?

Pain sliced through her as she curled her body into itself. *No!* She wouldn't let Peng's poisonous accusations taint what she believed in her heart. She loved Will. Yes, she'd only known him a short time, but he was everything she hadn't believed she wanted. Handsome, strong, rugged. And at the same time, he was good and kind and...and...a pirate. A man, by definition, a thief. A cunning, determined, self-serving, profit-driven thief.

Jun held her head. She wiped her mouth with the back of her hand. Ting brought a cool cloth to bath her face. Jun shivered as its chill joined the cold pit growing inside her. The chill of Will's deception would encase her heart in ice for the rest of her days.

She groaned. "Ting, how could I have been so wrong?"

Ting crouched next to her and wrapped an arm around her shoulders. "You are never wrong, Mistress. Please, tell me what has happened."

Jun realized she still held Will's logbook clenched tight to her stomach. She held it out to Ting. "I don't know what to believe anymore."

"Has Mister Will gone?"

The image of Peng's men dragging a bleeding Will from the hall flashed through her mind. "Yes, he's gone."

Ting gave her a small squeeze. "He will be back. You shouldn't worry. He loves you."

Jun lifted her eyes to Ting's. "How do you know?"

"I know. I see."

Jun pulled out of Ting's embrace and sat back. She opened the log to the back pages she'd read the night before, running her fingers over his words. "I thought I saw, too, but what if we were deceived?"

"No. I see when you look away. He still has love in his eyes for you."

"Maybe he's fooled us both." Jun flipped the book to the front. It all looked official enough. If he were lying about the *Scarlet Night*, why would he be so protective of this log? He'd hardly let it leave his sight. Running her thumb along the edges of the pages, she noticed gaps in the pages. There were sheets missing. Why would Will remove pages, unless the log was nothing more than a plant?

Jun quickly scanned the surrounding entries. "This is only dated months ago. By this, the *Scarlet Night* was traveling and raiding ships traveling south down the west side of Africa, then the pages for the next week are missing. But our information said the British held the ship…privateering has been repealed. Unless the whole log is a trick. But then why remove a week's worth of entries?" Jun flipped to another gap. "And more removed here." She stood, moved into a patch of sunlight, and lifted the book to look closer. "The dates don't appear altered. I don't understand." Jun mumbled to herself as she tried to make sense out of what she was looking at. "Why carry an incomplete log unless he was trying to hide something? Or confuse us?"

Ting turned to look at her. "Did you say, *Scarlet Night*, Mistress?"

Jun continued to examine the precise nature in which the missing pages were painstakingly cut away from the book. "Yes. That's what he told me."

She tapped the book. "This confirms the name at least, but was that the ship that wrecked on the reef?" She pulled at the bit of red sail. "Scarlet…red sails…" All of that made sense. "The wreckage on the beach…"

"That was my Dowd's ship."

Jun's mind churned with different scenarios. What if Will had been planted here as well? There had been no sign of any other survivors. Not even a single body. And the odd bits of wreckage… For a ship that size… Ting's words finally connected somewhere in her brain. "Wait. Did you say Dowd? *Your* Mister Dowd? Qi's father?"

"Aye. From a long time ago. He told me the stories."

"Are you sure he said the *Scarlet Night*?"

"I believe so, yes. He said he was on the crew of a grand ship with masts so tall they caught the bottoms of the clouds. So high, he said, he would sit with crows. The ship could sail quick as the wind, and when she battled, its cannons fired red smoke like the devil was rising from the water. They were famous and feared."

Jun shook her head. It sounded like a fanciful tale told to woo a young girl. Besides, it couldn't be the same ship. "But he's been with our fleet for more than five years."

"Yes. He's happy to fight for you, Mistress. Proud to be here. Loves Qi and me. Grateful you have been so kind to us."

Could the *Scarlet Night* have sailed these waters before? Jun struggled to remember. Her head pounded. If the *Scarlet* had pirated anywhere in the South China Seas or the Indian Ocean, she would have known of them before this. "Did Mister Dowd ever tell you how he came here?"

Ting smiled and nodded. "Oh, yes, mistress. He walked."

"Walked? Not sailed?"

"No. He told me he lost his fortune and nearly his life when he made a mistake to leave the big sea. Never would tell me how. But said he followed his heart east before being hired by a spice merchant. Took him a long time to travel. Says he walked a silk road straight to me."

"That would have taken years. How could he know what happened to the *Scarlet Night* since he left their crew?"

Ting lifted one shoulder. "I don't know, Mistress."

"What ship is he on now?"

"He sails with Commander—"

A great pounding came from within Jun's chamber seconds before Peng and six of his men barged through.

Jun slammed the book closed. "What do you think—"

"We are under attack." Peng grabbed her arm and tugged at her. "Three hundred ships. British, sailing from India. Heading down the strait to attack this island and deliver your head to the Chinese."

Will's log book fell to the ground. "Are you certain?"

Peng looked at her in exasperated disbelief. "Yes. You must leave *at once*. My men will escort you to your junk. I've alerted your crew. They stand at the ready. Every last man is prepared to protect you with their lives." He nodded to his men. "I do not want to start a panic until I know you are safely away. As soon as you sail, I'll send word into the village. We'll fill the ships that now lie in the harbor and get the others away. They will be safe. I give you my promise."

Jun looked back at a horrified Ting. "Ting....Qi."

"Yes, yes, I'll see to them, as well, and all those in the palace. You must leave now. *Go*."

"It's not right for me to leave like a thief in the night. I cannot leave my people to face this battle without me. If I've brought this threat down upon us—"

"How will you help them with your head on a spike and your entrails fed to the sharks?" Peng grabbed her upper arms. "Without you we are *all* lost. If you truly want to save your people, you will leave, and be alive tomorrow to lead us back from this devastating attack." He lowered his head and implored. "I will not watch while our enemy kills you. Please. Go."

Jun gave one final glance back at a tearful Ting. "Please, Mistress...we will join you soon...save yourself."

The six men surrounded Jun as she snatched her twin baldrics on the way out. Peng was right, inciting panic would be the worst thing to do right now, so she held her head high, and with a false determination strode through those gathering in the great hall and marched the short distance to board her ship.

With each step, she tried in vain to explain away Will's hand in this. She failed her people with her own selfish desires. The crushing pain in her heart was her reward for succumbing to her weakness. Her knuckles whitened as she tightened the grip on the wide straps of her baldrics. She'd never be so fooled again.

The proud junk waiting for her at its private dock had been Fu's pride. He had spared no expense when it came to the strength and beauty of his ship. Four masts rose straight into the blue of the brilliant afternoon. The shell-shaped, battened sails still sat folded like a woman's fan waiting for the order to be away. At her arrival, the crew scrambled into action. Ropes were untethered, the helmsmen took to the rudder. The lead sail was lowered and swung into place waiting to catch the wind.

Sunshine gleamed off the black-glossed rails with the pressed golden embellishments along the ship's sleek-lined bow. Fu always wanted to appear like a glimmering sun god rising out of the cold dark seas. Cinnabar fret work graced the upper doorframes while red silk flags fluttered their good luck along the masts to bring blessings from the great dragon.

Peng's men didn't allow her time to dally above deck, however. They moved her quickly below to the opulent quarters she once shared with her husband. Her eyes struggled to adjust to the sudden darkness after the brilliance of the day. The thick hull and intricate series of bulkheads below muffled the sounds of the harbor. She heard the creak of the door ahead, but where was the light? Her quarters had windows running along three sides.

Had they turned her around somehow? It hadn't been that long since she sailed on this ship. She practically lived aboard for years. How had she gotten lost?

"It's so dark, we've headed aft by mistake. This isn't my quarters." She reached out to touch the door. If she was mistaken, the door would boast a magnificent carving of a dragon. Jun couldn't see a damn thing—the men surrounding her moved in one lightning-fast, fluid movement. Strong hands wrenched the baldrics from her grip, while others issued a mighty shove propelling her forward. Jun grasped out in the darkness for something to keep her from falling flat on her face. "Fools! What do you think you're doing?" She screamed at them.

Before she could turn back on her assailants, Jun heard the door slam shut followed by the rusty scrape of a metal hasp. Anger, fear, and the sick cloying grip of realization wrapped around her.

Peng! It was him. He was the one. He was the betrayer…not Will.

Jun slammed her fists on the floor and roared into the darkness. It was that razor-faced, purple-assed bastard who was the traitor. And she had walked, head high, right into his trap.

Chapter 20

Jun pounded at the thick oak door as she felt the ship begin its move away from the dock, picking up speed as the sails caught the wind. The inner latch and door handle had been removed. It was pointless, to beat her hands raw, but as shock turned to white-hot anger, Jun screamed, reared back, and hurled herself against the door only to fall to the floor in pained frustration.

She groped along the edges of the room as her eyes began to adjust to the darkness. This was her quarters, but like the door handle, it had been thoroughly stripped of everything familiar.

Tables, Fu's desk, the rich lacquered chair where he used to sit. The bed had been removed. Wooden slates remained where she and Fu once slept. Gone were the rich wool rugs and the other spoils of their years of plunder. Even the oil lanterns had been wrenched from the walls. Brass strapping that once held them reached out like twisted, dead fingers. The wide panoramic sweep of beautiful leaded windows was now covered with thick wood panels. Jun clawed at them with all her strength, but they had been nailed into place and held firm.

One small knothole in one of the panels allowed a single slim shaft of daylight to slice through into the gloom. Jun held out her hand to catch the tiny struggling ray in her palm as her hope narrowed to that same pinhole.

As surely as the sun shone this day, Jun was dead unless she could come up with a way to get out of this room.

She'd been deceived and by the undeniable evidence now surrounding her, Peng had planned this deception and betrayal for quite some time. Had he hired and used Will as part of his evil plan? And then betrayed him as well in the great hall? Or had Will's arrival just played into his scheme?

Jun sank to the floor again and covered her face with her hands. She searched her memory for some sign she had missed along the way. Anything that would have alerted her to Peng's plot. Will couldn't have been part of this. That would be too much to bear.

No, this screamed of Peng's exhaustive attention to every possible detail. He was too thorough in his execution of even the smallest task. It was one of his traits she used to admire. Jun's anger raged. She'd make sure she was equally meticulous when she hung him by the balls and ripped his head off.

Jun's eyes slowly adjusted to the dark as she surveyed the emptiness surrounding her. What could have spurred him to go to such extremes? Peng had objected to her relationship to Will, but this was so far beyond a simple act of jealousy. Peng couldn't have executed all of this in so short a time.

No, her abduction had been cold and calculated. How had Peng managed to turn her own crew against her? She struggled to remember. They'd moved her below so quickly. Had it been her crew at the helm or had he changed out her men for his own?

Jun couldn't breathe. The air in the room was stale and thick with the heat of the day. Stifling. Sweat ran down the channel of her spine. She pulled at the thick leather strapping of her armor.

Ignore the heat. Think, damn it! She got to her feet and began pacing the length of the room. Her boots sounded muffled in the contained space. The only image that continued to circle in her thoughts was Peng's men knocking Will to the ground. A smear of blood upon the tiles. Was Will alive? Jun's heart ached at the thought. Peng was a cold ruthless killer. Yet another skill of his extensive training she once admired. But that was when he was doing her bidding. Now…she cringed at the extent of the brutality she knew he was capable of. If Peng wanted Will eliminated, the deed would already be done. Will would already be dead. A sob caught in her throat. She tore at her armor until it released and she cast it from her. The silk beneath clung to her skin.

And what about the rest? Would Qi and Ting be spared? Her village? Her advisors? How sweeping was this mutiny? Were Peng's men laying waste to them all? Executing them as she sat here, helpless to save them? And how long before she would meet her end like the rest?

The door swung open bringing a rush of cool air and Peng carrying a lantern and a pistol. He was alone and closed the door tight behind him.

"You wasted no time," Jun spun on him. "I've barely settled into my new quarters." Her rush to attack him was halted by the dark barrel of his gun pointed at her face.

"I've wasted years," he sneered. "But no more. It is my time now. I've worked everything out to the tiniest detail." His free hand swept the empty room. "And it was so much simpler than I imagined getting you here. Thank you for that."

Jun's back teeth were threatening to crumble under the tension in her jaw. All she needed was one slip. One flaw in his movements. She narrowed her eyes and watched, waited. "How long have you been planning this ridiculous plot?"

Peng lifted one shoulder. "What does that matter? And it could only be deemed ridiculous if it hadn't succeeded so brilliantly."

"Brilliant is not what I'd call this, but I applaud your dedication. It must have taken months to arrange. How did you ever manage to turn my entire fleet against me?"

"Oh, no, no…" Peng shook his head and gave her a pitying look. "On the contrary. You are still much loved by all. I'm counting on your fleet's loyalty. Fighting so many would be foolish. No, fear not, your reign may be over, but your sterling legend will live on forever."

The glib tone to his words scratched like iced claws down her skin, but he would never see her fear. She'd never give him the satisfaction. "How do you plan on getting away with this?"

"Easy. I'm using your lover." Peng waved the pistol at her. Did that mean Will lived? Jun tried to keep her emotions in check. Peng would use any advantage.

He continued to gloat. "How fortuitous for me that he arrived when he did. I imagine it would have been weeks more planning had he not washed up on our shores and given me the perfect opportunity to conclude my plot against you." Peng stroked his beard. "Soon everyone will know he came to our waters only to worm his way into your good graces so he could ultimately kill you for the bounty on your head. He was a fraud. A British spy sent to kill you. Being a weak woman, of course, you fell for his lies. I tried to caution you. It was I who saw through his deceit and continued to warn you against him, but you wouldn't listen. Refused my sage counsel, and that is what led to your demise.

"When you finally discovered his treachery, you ordered his death, of course, but not before he confessed that his shipwreck had all been staged. There was no ship lost in the storm. The wreckage on the beach had been planted here. He warned you his men waited for him off the coast of Salahnama."

Peng shook his head at her and ticked his tongue. "So ashamed you had been taken in, you refused to believe he had gotten the better of you. To save face, you pig-headedly sailed into the very ambush he'd warned you about. You were taken prisoner and tortured mercilessly by our enemies."

He laid a hand on his chest. "I tried to stop you, of course. Convince you to send your men instead. But your stubborn nature has always been your fatal weakness, Jun. You wouldn't listen to reason. I even took my own ship to chase after you. But alas, I was too late. We defeated the threat against us, of course, but we were too late to save you. You died gloriously in my arms, bloodied and beaten, but not before you graced me with your crown. A final gift for all my years of loving devotion. Trusting me to take your fleet, and honor your wishes to make us the most powerful force in the world."

Chilled sweat rolled down her temples. "No one will believe this."

"They already do." He smiled. "You will die the sad misguided hero, which is more than you deserve. But your tragic, brutal death will tighten the resolve of the fleet, and their anger and revenge will stoke the fires of our crews. We'll be unstoppable."

"Why, Peng?" She swept her arms to the sides. "Why go to all this trouble? You are the second in command. Why turn on me now when I have given you so much already? Made you my first mate. Gave you a position of honor amongst my men. Why would you—"

"Because it all should have been mine from the beginning." Peng pounded a fist to his chest. "*I* should have inherited the fleet. I should have taken Fu's place in *every* way." He pointed the pistol into her face, his eyes wild. "But you marched in after his death like a bloody fool wearing his bloody armor and took what was *mine*." Spittle formed in the corners of his mouth. "Even then I had hoped that you would in time come to join with me and we would rule together. So I humbled myself while you played the great ice empress. I sacrificed everything to serve you. How many times did I bow and scrape and kiss your hems. I offered you my life—my heart—and time after time you rejected me. You may have fooled the rest into believing your own propaganda, but you were *never* a queen in my eyes. Some may have forgotten what you are, but not I." He sneered in disgust as his gaze raked over her.

A thick vein stood out on his forehead. Jun remained coldly silent. Letting him have his rant. Hoping to find some hole in his insane reasoning. Waiting for any chance.

Peng was silent for a long moment as he gathered himself. When he spoke again his anger had been replaced by something even more sinister. His tone was low. Chilling. "I've seen you. Watched you when you escaped into your precious garden sanctuary and thought you were alone. I've become quite adept at sneaking into the shadows. When you slip into your daily bath, I'm there. Finding *my* pleasure within a perfect hiding place. Hidden away to…entertain myself not ten feet from the sight of your tub.

Fu confided in me one drunken night. He built the room behind the carved walls. It was a particular fetish of his as well to spy on you. Didn't he tell you? All those times…watching. But then Fu was gone and in this, at least, I took his place. And there was no one to stop me."

Bile rose in Jun's throat. She began to shake.

"I've seen you let down your hair. Heard the small satisfied sigh you breathed when you lowered yourself into the water. I know the exact shape of your perfect breasts and how brazenly you slide the soap over your nipples. And how the water sluices over your thighs when you raise your leg to wash."

Jun couldn't feel her hands. His admission paralyzed her.

He waved the pistol lower. "At first I was repulsed to see that hideous flower covering your filthy cunt, but then it was all I could picture when I imagined you pleasuring yourself beneath the water. Your teasing fingers plucking at those garish pinked petals."

It was all Jun could do not to cover herself as if she stood naked before him now. The cold numbing shock was giving way to a slow hot fury, however. The flames of her anger began to burn deep in her belly.

Peng's eyes hardened. "But now you've spread your legs for *him*. A deaf man. An inferior westerner. A cursed man who washed up on our shores like a piece of discarded filth from the sea. And still you lay with him. Took him into your *sainted* bed. Sainted, ha! The great Jian Jun. Convincing everyone of her chaste life. Playing the grieving widow. The pure innocent. Ha." He moved closer, jammed the barrel of the gun hard under her chin and spit into her face. "Once a whore, always a whore. Fu should have left you where he found you."

Jun held his hateful gaze for a long moment. If she had her blade she would have split him open from his crotch to his skull. Instead, she forced herself not to blink. Furious tears washed her eyes.

She used them.

"I-I never knew, Peng. You never told me how you felt. I only took Will into my bed because I was so desperately lonely. Had you given me some idea of your feelings. Come to me." She laid a hand on his arm, but removed it when he put more pressure on the pistol at her throat. "Fu's voyeurism excited me. If you had let me know you shared his obsession, I could have danced for you like I did for him." It took all she had not to gag on the words. "We could have been together. Been discreet. It's not too late. You could stop all this nonsense. Turn this ship around. We could go back. Rule the empire together. As one. Side by side." The lies turned to dust on her tongue. If she could play on his sick mania…get him to lower the pistol for just a moment…

He laughed and shoved her away from him. "Why would I ever want you now? I don't want some used cast-off whore. And after what I found, I certainly don't *need* you anymore. While you were busy fucking Captain Quinn, I was learning all I needed to know about how he made his way to our threshold. I discovered his secret."

Peng fished into his pocket and pulled out sheets of paper. Jun recognized them at once. He waved the stolen pages from Will's log in her face. "I'll be the one to open up the world to our mighty force. I've uncovered the mystery guarding the west. Found a safe passage to unleash the Dragon's Fire on the rest of the world." He notched his chin. "It will *all* be mine."

"Your people will hail *me* as their hero. In time, you'll be an afterthought scribbled in the depths of some moldy history book while I will be proclaimed as the most powerful ruler to have ever lived."

The corruption of his brain was complete. The hairs on the back of her neck stood on end. It was frightening to behold such a twisted sense of reality. There had to be a way to stop him. Jun's hands curled into fists. "You'll never get away with this."

Peng laughed at her. "I already have."

She swung her arms wide "Then please, I beg you, end this. If you're going to kill me, what are you waiting for? Finish your perfectly planned plot. Shoot me."

"So impatient." Peng scratched at his beard. "I've waited for this moment for so long. Years. You must allow me to savor it." He smiled a chilling smile. "Why not enjoy myself? I've earned this moment. But like any plot, it's best when the plan is allowed to be fluid like the sea. Able to ebb and flow with the whim of fate. Much more enjoyable that way. Don't you agree?" He didn't give her a chance to answer before continuing. "I was going to order my men to kill Captain Quinn the moment I seized him, but then *you* promised to take his head yourself. I couldn't help but get a wonderful idea. I wonder, would you still remove his head if it meant you'd save your own neck?"

The air rushed from her lungs. A thin ray of hope sliced through the darkness. "He's still alive."

"For now." He tipped his head and studied her. "Don't look so pleased. I suppose it wasn't much of a bargain, knowing I'm going to kill you anyway. No bother. I'll do your dirty work for you. Again." Peng returned to the door and gave it two quick knocks. "I've been doing it for years. You've enjoyed waving that judgmental hand of yours and making me carry out your cruel punishments with every flick of your pale wrist while you kept the blood from your own hands." The door opened and Peng moved to leave. "It's about time you appreciated just how vile I can be for you, my *queen*. It will be quite a lengthy show. You should rest up."

Peng's slow smile sent ice through Jun's veins. "I give you my promise, you will see your precious Captain Quinn once more before I slice him into bite-sized morsels for the sharks. You'll have to wait just a bit longer to reunite, however. I've decided to give him a bit of a show as well. I do hope he likes surprises."

Chapter 21

Will woke with his face in filth and his head trying to pound its way off his shoulders. *What the bloody hell?* He fingered the tender swelling at the base of his skull before the room started to spin. Closed his eyes, he tried to get his bearings. His stomach roiled. Where the hell was he? What was the last thing he could remember?

Jun. Jun's face peering at him around the back of that bastard Chou Peng. As four men blindsided him. Will's head felt like they'd tried to cleave it in two. What had they hit him with? A cannonball?

He struggled to sit, and cranked open one eye. Thankfully the room ceased spinning. Will placed his hands flat on the floor. The room may have stopped twirling, but he knew rocking when he felt it. Wherever he was, he was back on the water.

The ship wasn't moving, however. Anchored, not moored, by the gentle yaw of the bow. Still, without knowing how long they'd extinguished his lights, he had no way of knowing where they'd taken him. He could be forty feet from shore or forty miles.

One thing he was certain of, he was in a cell. Iron bars made up one wall. Will curled his lip at the stagnant odor of unwashed bodies and fetid straw. They'd thrown him on a prison barge. By the pungent smell, he wasn't the first inhabitant, nor the only.

He tried to stand, but the violent spinning returned. Maybe they hit him with the whole cannon. Will closed his eyes again as darkness closed over him.

When he opened his eyes once more, what little light penetrated this lower deck had shifted. Hours must have passed. Damn it, he needed to stay conscious if he was ever going to figure how the hell to get out of here. At least the pounding in his head had lessened some to just a blinding throb.

Slowly, Will made it to his feet without passing out or throwing up. Things were looking up. He moved to the bars and peered out. Cells lined the outer walls of the ship. It was difficult to see into the murky depths, but he could just make out the bare, filthy feet of one occupant and the curled figure of another.

The air closer to the door was only slightly better. Will tested the door by tugging at it. Nothing gave even slightly. The bars were solid and a thick block lock showed no sign of weakness. He slid down the bars to sit again.

Will blew out a breath. The last time he'd been in a cell like this, he'd been on his way to get his neck stretched by the British. Images of the heads he'd seen in the village reminded him that the Dragon's Fire Fleet didn't go in much for hanging. Shorter corpses were all the rage here. Loppings were more their style. What were the odds he'd pull his arse out of this mess? Death was an angry bastard, and he'd already cheated him out of his soul more times than he could remember. Odds were slim this time.

But where was Jun in all of this? His capture had happened too fast back in the great hall. One minute he'd been heading to confront her about the missing pages of his logbook, and the next he'd been tasting the floor tiles.

Will frowned, trying to bring up the image of Jun's face in his mind's eye. Had it been surprise he'd seen? Fear? Fear for him? For herself? He'd only glimpsed her for a sliver of a moment. But here he sat. Was it by her order that he'd been locked up? Had she taken his anger as aggression toward her? Had this been her plan all along?

She had to know he'd never hurt her. Regardless of what she'd done with his log. Even if it were true that she used him only to warm her bed so she could gain information. Yes, he'd be devastated that once again he'd let his heart lead him into a doomed-from-the-dock relationship, but it wasn't the first time he'd been fooled by a beautiful face.

If he could just see her again. Scribble on a hunk of slate and ask her to tell him the whole story. If it were true that she'd coldly used him, he wanted to know. Better that than holding on to some misguided illusions. *Bloody hell. Look around you, you sorry bastard.* This sure as hell screamed of some cold-as-ice manipulations. They didn't call Jian Jun the Ice Empress for nothing.

He leaned his aching head against the bars and closed his eyes. Maybe losing his head wouldn't be the worst thing.

Something solid hit his shoulder. Will's eyes snapped open and he peered out into the dim space. A rough ball of straw-wrapped dung rolled away from the bars. Had some scurvy-arsed bilge rat thrown *shit* at him?

A man a few cells from his peered at him through the bars. In his hand, he held another straw ball. *Son of a bitch!* Wide eyes stared out at Will from a grimy bearded face. Will gave him the universal sign of the one-fingered salute as he stood to move away from the bars.

When the man waved his arms wildly at Will, he stopped and peered closer. Then the man dropped the ball he held and used his hand to tap at his shoulder, *'Captain?'*

The air punched out of Will's lungs. He gripped tight to the bars and squinted to see better through the murk. The man called out to the cells on either side of him. The other occupants scrambled to their doors. The first man pointed at Will and signed *'Captain'* once more.

Was he seeing things? How…? It couldn't be. *Griffin?* And the man next to him was a ragged, beaten Simon Hills, his helmsman. It took him a moment longer to recognize the third man as part of his face was obscured by a darkened bandage. It was Higgins, the quartermaster from the *Scarlet Night.*

They'd survived the wreck? His heart tried to race out of his chest. Will scrubbed his hand over his eyes before trusting what he was seeing. Survivors. He tugged in vain on the bars of his cell. Who else had made it? Were there more here? He held tight to the reins of his hope. Could Tupper be among them? Will quickly signed to Griffin. *'How many of you?'*

Griffin pointed to them and held up three fingers. That was it. No more. The wound of his heart burned with a renewed sting. It was a long shot. Still, the rush of joy at seeing these few members of his crew filled Will's soul. He hadn't been the only one. Will held his forehead. He'd given up all hope. Thank God, he'd been wrong. Who knows? There could be more of them out there.

Will shook his finger at Griffin. *'Where are we? How did you get here?'*

'Pulled from the sea after the wreck. Locked us up straight away. Think we're spies.' Griffin spelled the last word.

'Who?' Will asked, even though he knew the answer.

'Dragon's Fire. Sailed straight into the dragon's den. Told us Jian Jun wouldn't let us live.' Griffin struggled to spell the words he didn't have gestures for. *'Scuttled what was left of the* Night.*'*

'Didn't the ship break up on the reef? What was left?'

'Did hit the reef. Hard. Shattered the bow. Opened us clean to the forward mast. Listed hard to starboard. Taking on water by the barrel load, but the aft got hung up on the coral.'

Will hesitated, but he had to ask again. *'Tupper?'*

Griffin gave a slight shake to his head. *'Saw her go down. Rode the bowsprit straight into the waves.'*

Will swallowed hard. How much confirmation did he need? Did he have to see her waterlogged corpse to believe she was truly gone? *'The others?'*

Griffin shook his head again and gestured. *'Waves tore us apart. You know what the seas were like. We were the lucky ones.'* He slammed a palm against the bars. *'Lucky, my arse. Locked up like an animal. Waiting for dragon lady to swing her bloody sword. Would have rather gone down with the blasted ship.'*

Will agreed. Another thing Griffin had signed nagged at him. *'Said they scuttled the rest?'*

'After they dragged our sorry hides out of the drink, their men took what they could salvage, dozen chests, barrels, whatever they could carry. Waves were still high when they came about and leveled the guns. Blew the rest of the Scarlet *to bits.'*

Will frowned. If Jun's men stripped the ship of all its plunder, why the hell had they gathered a small pile of rubble on the beach for him to sift through? He looked back at Griffin.

He was still signing. *'Dragged us aboard this barge. Been here since.'*

'You're sure it was Jian Jun's men?'

Griffin nodded. *'That's what they said.'*

'Did you see her?'

'No. Told we would see her just before she killed us.' Griffin made sharp, hard signs. *'Heard she's an ugly bitch.'*

The rush to defend Jun surged through him. Jun's image lingered in his mind's eye. Will didn't take the time to explain to Griffin that "ugly bitch" couldn't have been more wrong. Her beauty would steal his breath away. However, the question of her role in the capture of his surviving crew and the rest still gnawed at Will. He scrubbed at his jaw. None of this was adding up.

Will signed to Griffin again. *'Officers?'*

'One or two. Took their orders from a...' Griffin stopped to spell. *'p-u-r-p-l-e man.'*

Peng. It had to be him. Will ran a hand over his forehead. The more he heard the less things made sense. If Jun had known about Griffin and the others, why wouldn't she tell him? And why would she go through all the trouble of arranging an insignificant pile of wreckage for him to inspect? If they'd helped themselves to the ship's bounties before they scuttled it, why leave him anything? Certainly they would have recognized the log box as valuable. Why bother giving it back to him at all?

His head throbbed with the effort to figure it all out.

Another ball of shit hit Will in the thigh. He glared at Griffin. *'Will you stop throwing shit at me.'*

   'Trying to get your attention.'

Will shook his upturned hand at Griffin. *'What?'*

'Where have you been all this time?'

Good question. Will jerked back, as if he'd been slapped. Where had he been and with whom? Had everything been an elaborate lie? And for what reason? God, his head hurt. Will rubbed a hand over his eyes before answering the man.

Slowly, he signed, *'I'm not sure.'*

Chapter 22

Will paced his cage and kicked at the regiment of rats that scurried along the filthy walls. The longer he pondered, however, the less sense he made of everything he'd learned.

Griffin, Hills, and Higgins had been here almost two weeks. If the plan was to kill them, what were they waiting for? From all he'd observed, justice was swift among Jun's numbers. Why the hesitation? And why hadn't Will joined what remained of his crew when he'd washed ashore? They captured him quickly enough. He still had sand caked on his face when they dragged him in to the great hall that first day. Why then the pretense of giving him his own quarters along with the freedom to come and go? True, they had set that cabbage-reeking tail on him. Did they think he would reveal some plot against them?

And why…why would Jun allow him so deeply into her life? Into her bed if they believed him to be a threat to her? Still hoping he'd reveal something? Did they suspect he could talk after all? In his sleep?

As angry and confused as he was, Will couldn't rid his mind of the last time he and Jun had been together. In the filth of his cell, the light fading on the day, Will couldn't help but remember their nights. Feeding each other and making love in the garden surrounded by the beauty of the plants and the heady scent of the flowers. Jun's gentle hand leading him to her bed. Slowly taking his clothes off.

She'd enchanted him last night. Settling him between her thighs. Taking him into the slick heat of her body while he braced himself over her to keep from crushing her. Her beautiful legs wrapped tight around his waist. The rhythm of his hips pushing him deeper and deeper into her with each thrust. Looking down into her flushed face as she rocked beneath him, signing '*More…more…more*' until his body couldn't contain his passion another moment and poured into her.

If all of that had been faked, he bloody well deserved to lose his head.

A shaft of lantern light caught Will's attention as someone moved between the cells. They'd already received their meal of maggot-ridden bread and piss water. Was it time for dessert?

The man was dressed in the cotton changshan of a native, but the short curly hair on his head debated that assumption.

Lifting the lantern high, the man made his way past the occupied cells, peering in at their sleeping occupants, almost as if he were searching for someone.

When he came to Will's cell, he startled to find Will awake, and standing so close to the bars. He pulled back in shock, but held the lantern closer to Will, squinting at him.

Will blinked against the light's assault. Who the hell was this?

As the question formed in Will's mind the man's jaw went slack. His mouth moved as he said something, then he held up one hand, crossed his thumb over his palm and tapped the outer corner of his eyebrow with his fingertips.

Bloody hell, the bastard just called me Bump!

Behind him, Will saw Griffin get up and peer out between the bars of his cell, then say something. The man before Will turned and exchanged some words with Griffin. Soon, Hills and Higgins were on their feet as well.

Will slammed his palm against the bars to get the man's attention. When he turned back, Will studied his face. He looked familiar somehow, but he couldn't recall how he might know the stranger. He was definitely a westerner. And he obviously knew Will…or at least he knew him as Bump.

The man in front of him, signed, *'It's me.'*

Bloody hell, that wasn't helping him. Will stared at him again.

He signed, *'A slow arm.'*

Will shook his head in frustration. What the hell?

The man gestures were hesitant and clumsy. *'Don't remember how to chicken.'*

Will pointed to Griffin and gestured. *'Do you know what he's trying to say?'*

Griffin spoke to the man and translated. *'He says it's been a long time. He can't remember how to talk to you.'*

'Who the fuck is he?'

The man pointed to Will's fingers and laughed. *'I know fuck. I remember fuck,'* he signed.

Griffin asked the man a question. The man turned back to Will and spelled. *'d-o,'* he frowned and raised three fingers, *'w-d.'* He gave Will a quick, satisfied nod.

'*Who?*' Will looked back to Griffin in question.

Griffin spelled it quicker. '*D-o-w-d.*'

It was Will's turn to pull back in shock and let his jaw go slack. It had to have been close to fifteen years. He peered at the man. Recognition finally registered with his brain. He'd been with the *Scarlet* crew since before the great earthquake of ninety-two.

Son of a bitch. They'd been gangly teenagers then. Dowd was the bloke that hurled his guts every time Ric Robbins ordered him to climb into the crow's nest. He'd been one of the handful of crew to have stayed on the ship and survived the earthquake. And somehow because of his harrowing brush with death, he grew into a reckless, horny bastard that chased everything in a corset. He left the *Night* to rut under the skirts of some Italian merchant's daughter if Will's memory was right. How the hell had he gotten here?

Will pointed, '*I remember you.*'

'*You better, you sorry excuse for a big bosom.*'

Will begged Griffin, '*Please get him to stop signing. He just called me a giant tit. Ask him how he got here? Last I saw him we were sailing off the coast of Portugal.*'

It took Griffin a minute to get all the information, but only a few gestures to translate. '*Man's a horndog.*'

Will nodded. '*Tell me something I don't already know.*'

'*Chased one woman after another. Daughters of spice merchants. Wives of silk traders. Worked the silk road. Met a beautiful Chinese girl. Got her pregnant. Now he sails with the Dragon's Fire.*' Griffin listened some more. '*Questions came down through the fleet. Asking about* Scarlet Night. *Heard there were prisoners. Close to home port, he transferred to another ship to reach Pandang. See his wife, daughter. See if he knew any of the prisoners. Find out what happened to the ship.*'

With Griffin's help, Will asked Dowd for news from Pandang. Had he heard anything more about them around the fleet?

'*No. Things are strange in the village.*'

A wave of unease washed over Will. Impatience at the translation back and forth rose until he wanted to reach through the bars and shake the man. '*Strange how?*'

'*Tension is high. Too many ships packed into the harbor. Lots of soldiers roaming streets. Can't find his wife. No one has seen her. She works directly for Jian Jun. Refused entry. None have seen her either. Not since dawn. Nothing is disturbed at his wife's home. Like they just disappeared.*'

Will's eyebrows raised. '*You're Qi's father.*'

Dowd didn't need Griffin to translate. *'You know Qi?'*
Will nodded. *'And Ting.'*
'Where are they?'
His earlier wave of unease turned into a tidal wave. Will pressed a hand
to his stomach as his gut twisted. *'I don't know. Griffin, translate.'* Will
was quick to explain seeing Ting and Qi last night, and being seized this
morning. They were safe and well the last time he saw them all, but he
was concerned. If Ting and Qi and Jun were all missing, it was more than
likely Peng had something to do with it.
'Do you mean Chou Peng? General Chou?'
Will nodded.
*'Ting dislikes him. Doesn't trust him. He's been cruel to Qi when he
thinks no one sees.'* Dowd confessed.
The tidal wave crashed over his head. Anger had Will reaching through
the bars and grabbing for Dowd's chest. *'Get us out of here. We'll help
you find them.'*
Dowd shook his head. *'You're crazy. Even if I could get you off this
ship, the village is full of Peng's muscle.'*
Will shoved at Dowd. *'I think he has done something with Ting and
Qi. If I can talk to Jian Jun she'll know where they are. I know a secret
passageway into her private quarters.'*
Dowd held up his hands as if to surrender. *'If they catch me, I'm dead.'*
'Better you than Qi.'
The man's jaw hardened. A dark glare crossed over his face. *'If
he's touched her...'*
Will's hope rekindled. Dowd may have been a confirmed womanizer
in the past, but it was clear he loved his daughter and would defend
her with his life.
*'Find the keys and bring them to me, then get yourself away. I'll take
care of the rest. We'll meet you on the north side of the palace, by the walled
gardens.'* Will patted the man's shoulder. *'I promise you, we'll find her.'*
Dowd's throat worked before he nodded and signed. *'You're not far
from shore, but you'll have to swim.'*
'I've done that before.' He held the man's concerned stare a moment
longer. *'Come on, time's wasting. We need the cover of night if we're going
to get out of here.'*
*'You don't know how swift the punishment for disobedience is. I could
be dead before you hit the water and then who would find my family?'*
'They'll never know it was you.' Will reached out and lowered the flame
on the lantern. *'Douse that light, get me the keys, and get the hell away*

from here. You have my word, I'll never tell a soul.'

Dowd reached through the bars and shook Will's hand. They exchanged no words after that. No signs or gestures. They didn't need to. Dowd would help them. Time and distance would never diminish the fact that they had once been loyal shipmates. Fought battles together. They would still stand back to back and fight for one another now. It was part of the code.

Darkness blanketed the deck. Will swallowed his instinctual anxiety. Cold beads of sweat formed on his forehead. Closing his eyes, he could picture the layout in his mind. He would stand here until he had the key in his hand, then he would praise the darkness.

Will leaned against the bars. *Hurry Dowd.* As his mind had done since the day he washed up on the shores of Pandang, he instantly thought of Jun. Her image floated through his mind of its own accord.

He ground his teeth together. As soon as Dowd had told him Ting, Qi, and Jun hadn't been seen since early that morning, a sick twist had begun in his stomach. All the doubts, all the speculation surrounding his thoughts of any manipulation on Jun's part soured and threatened to eat a hole through his belly.

How could he have questioned what happened between them? This was Peng's doing. It all started to make sense. With what Griffin told him, Peng's men had captured the survivors of the *Scarlet Night* and Peng had taken what he could before scuttling the ship. He was stealing from Jun and had rigged the "discovery" of the ship's wreckage to throw her off the track of his deceit.

Will had fallen into the trap as well. He should have trusted his instincts when he saw those men meeting with Peng that morning. He'd known they were up to something, but had no proof to bring his accusations to Jun. He must have gotten too close for comfort. Otherwise he wouldn't be sharing a room with the rats.

And the logbook. Will hadn't figured out when Peng stole the pages, but it would make sense if he was plotting something against Jun. The information contained on those pages would come in mighty handy, but he couldn't mysteriously produce pages without first establishing the presence of the logs. He must have realized what he had from the bounty of the *Night* and concocted the entire scenario. Will had played right into his bony hands, and now he had Jun.

Come on Dowd. Where the hell are you?

Chapter 23

A hand touched Will's shoulder in the dark before Dowd fumbled a ring of heavy iron keys into his hands. There had to be twenty. Will reached out to thank Dowd, but his reach hit air. He wasted no time in starting the methodical task of testing each one, careful not to let them rattle. He might not be able to hear them, but surer than shit, the guards would.

Blood pumped through the veins in his neck. The sweat rolled past his temples. *No, not this one. Try the next. No…next. No…next. Yes.*

The key hit its mark. Will felt the lock click open. Adrenaline rushed through his limbs. He was free. Keeping his bearings, he turned and walked toward Griffin's cell until his foot hit bars. A hand met his. In the dark it could have been any of the three, but he passed the keys along and followed the line of cells to the door. Will didn't wait. He eased the latch, and opened the door a crack. Ah, blessed light.

Hills joined him, and then the others. Together they made their way toward the galley way leading to the upper decks. All of Will's senses— those that worked—were on high alert. He felt naked without a weapon and cursed himself every time he reached for one. What he wouldn't give for a blade. He made a move to start up the steps, but Griffin pulled him back into the shadows seconds before one of the guards started down the stairs.

Higgins was quick to strike, snapping the man's neck in one swift motion. The man was dead before his boot heel hit the last step. Hills relieved the dead man of his pistol. Higgins claimed his sword. Griffin nodded to them and jerked his chin up the stairs. They'd now take the lead.

Popping their heads above deck like some odd band of rabbits coming up from their hole, the four men moved unseen from the head of the stairs to a cluster of barrels lashed to the port rails.

Will looked over the side. It was a long way down to the black of the water. The lights of the village danced on the tips of the waves, but Dowd had been right. They were in for a bit of a swim. The problem wasn't going to be getting them to shore, the challenge was going to be getting them all into the water without so much as a splash.

Farther down the deck was a perfectly coiled rope, beyond that stood another stack of crates. Will waited for his chance, then stepped out of the shadows and moved unhurriedly past the rope, grabbed the top spiral, and threw it behind his back and over the rail.

Ducking behind the crates, he watched as the rope quickly unwound, gravity pulling its length over the side. Bits of hemp clouded around the edge of the rail. To his relief the rope's end was cleated halfway up the mast. The rasping of the hemp against the side had caught the attention of one of the crew, however. The man approached the odd positioning of the rope to investigate.

Hills and Higgins struck once more. A barrel pressed to a temple followed by a slash of a blade and the man wouldn't be investigating anything else ever again. This man carried no pistol, but his cutlass and short boarding ladder were gratefully accepted by Griffin and Will. A body in a pool of blood was sure to be discovered sooner than later. It was time they were away.

Will was the first over the rail. Winding one leg around the rope, he was able to descend one handed rather than holding the boarding blade between his teeth.

Cold water filled his boots as he eased himself into the gentle waves. *Damn it to hell.* He just bought these boots. After a soak in saltwater, they'd never be the same.

Kicking off away from the ship, Will made his way along the shadowed side of the junk before heading directly for the village. They could come ashore a few yards up the beach into the undergrowth. He'd figure out their next move from there.

Luck was with them. Dowd had been right. Ships of every description crowded the docks. Given a running start, Will could have crossed the harbor and never hit water. The junks were packed in tighter than salted herring in a barrel. That meant the village was full as well with all manner of strangers. Still four westerners were bound to cause unwanted interest, but just then Griffin pointed back to the ship they'd left and signed *'Alarm. Found the guards. No time to debate. Let's move.'*

The commotion caused by the alarm was the perfect opportunity for the group to slip through the crowd rushing toward the beach and make their way to the north side of the palace.

Adrenaline pumped through Will. He practically danced with impatience.

Where the hell was Dowd? No sooner had Will had the thought when the man stepped from the shadows. Will jerked his head telling him to follow him. Griffin, Hills, and Higgins would wait and cover them from the back.

Will found the row of shrubs Qi had shown him. He pulled Dowd after him. The branches caught in his hair and snagged on his clothing. He was a hell of a lot bigger than a five-year-old. Getting through Qi's secret tunnel might be harder than he anticipated. He clawed his way through the narrow passage.

Peering into the garden, no lanterns burned. Rock and brush scraped at his skin as he forced his way in. Once there, he waited for Dowd as he scanned the garden for any signs of life. The difference in the look of the gardens with the long dark shadows reaching through the plantings chilled his damp skin. Had it only been a single day since he'd been here with Jun? Dread clawed at his belly. If Peng had done something to hurt her... or Qi and Ting.

Dowd joined him. Blood ran from a scratch down his cheek. He smeared at it with the back of his hand before signing, *'Where do we go?'*

Will tipped his head then led him closer to Jun's private chambers. He paused and gestured to Dowd, *'Do you hear anything?'*

Dowd shook his head. When Will turned to continue inside, Dowd stopped him with a hand to his arm. *'You made a mistake. Said Qi told you about getting into the garden.'*

Will nodded.

Dowd frowned at him. *'You meant Ting.'*

'No. It was Qi.'

Dowd shook his head. *'Impossible. How?'*

'No time to explain.'

'Try.' Dowd's stare was intent. Something had indeed happened to this man when that little girl came into his life. Will could read the love he had for the child in his gaze.

"Qi is kind. Sweet. Smart. Doesn't speak because she cannot hear.'

For the second time that night, Will watched the man's jaw go slack. He nodded to him when Dowd looked at him with a million questions reflected in his eyes.

'Later. Let's find her.'

Will moved up the path. Cold water still squished between his toes and wet the stones. He watched for any clue that would tell him what happened. Where they could be. Maybe Peng had moved them. Jun's new pipa sat exactly where she had left it the night before. The table was clear. If they'd left they did it in a hurry. They'd taken nothing with them.

When they reached Jun's sleeping chamber, Will noticed the blankets piled on the floor in the corner. Had the bed been stripped, wouldn't the covers be closer to the bed? Why were they clear across the room?

Candle smoke. Will lifted his nose and sniffed. The smell lingered in the air. The candle Jun lit last night sat in the same place, yet the wax was still warm, and liquid at the top.

Will crossed to the corner of the room and lifted the blankets from the floor.

Ting clutched a wide-eyed Qi to her chest. The child flew into Will's arms when she saw him and buried her head into his shoulder. Relief flooded Will as he held tight to the shaking child.

Dowd was beside him in a minute, pulling Ting to her feet and into his arms. The woman wept on his chest. He held her tight, kissing the top of her head, stroking her hair.

The chill of dread was quick to douse the relief Will was feeling. He searched the room over Qi's shoulder. Where was Jun? He lifted Qi's face from his chest and wiped at the tears from her cheeks. *'What happened? Where is Jun?'*

Qi's face scrunched up. She didn't understand. In his rush, he'd used signs he hadn't taught her yet.

'Jun.' She knew that sign. He shrugged his shoulders and scanned the room as if looking for her and shrugged again. Qi was quick to scramble out of his arms and out of the room. Will interrupted Dowd and Ting.

'Ask her what happened? Where's Jun?'

Before Ting could answer Qi returned with a stick and berries. She mashed them and smeared their juice on the stick.

Peng. The purple berries on the stick were Peng. Qi threw the stick across the room and peered up at him with worry.

An icy hand of fear reached into Will's gut. Peng took Jun.

Dowd confirmed what Qi had already told him. *'He has her. Peng told her three hundred ships were coming for her. Sailed away on her junk. Hours ago. Soldiers poured in and took control of the village. Peng followed Jun away. They could be to Singapore by now.'*

'They're not in Singapore. Bet my life on it. Assure them there is no attack coming.' There was a reason Peng hadn't killed him yet. Why Hills and Griffin and Higgins still lived. He didn't know what twisted plan Peng had in mind, but there was no chance he simply sailed off with Jian Jun.

Will's hands curled into fists. He'd find her or die trying. Will turned to Dowd. *'I'll need your help. I don't know the first thing about sailing a junk. But I do know a thing or two about stealing one.'*

Chapter 24

Hunger gnawed at Jun's belly. Her thirst made her tongue feel swollen in her mouth. The oppressive heat in the closed cabin rose through the long hours of the afternoon, but now that the sun had set, the coolness against her sweat drenched clothing was making her teeth rattle.

Perhaps Peng's plan was to kill her slowly.

She curled into the side of the ship and shivered. Dying wasn't the worst thing. Jun hadn't lived this dangerous, violent life without facing death on more than a few occasions. Death didn't frighten her. There were even times in her life she'd wished for it.

But dying at Peng's hand, because of his treachery, that would not be a death she would willingly embrace.

Jun ran her fingertips over the dryness of her lips. Tears pinched the backs of her eyes when she remembered the feel of Will's kisses. The way he would angle his mouth and brush his lips over hers for a single stolen breath before capturing them. She could have kissed his beautiful mouth forever.

One tear slipped from the corner of her eye, Jun swiped at it in anger. Tears made her weak. If she was going to die, she would scratch and claw to her last breath. She feared for Will more than herself. At least she would see him before Peng did his worst. She'd be able to tell Will she loved him even if they couldn't find a way to beat Peng. Somehow, she'd tell Will that she'd loved him from the moment he gazed up at her with those stunning topaz eyes. She'd find a way to say the words even if she had to write it in her own blood. He would know her heart before either of them left this world. She'd make him understand.

Jun pulled her knees to her chest and shook with a mixture of heartache and determination. Peng could have it all. Her empire. Her palace. Her world. But he would never have the one thing he proclaimed to covet.

He'd never have her heart.

Chills continued to wrack her body. By the time Peng returned, Jun thought her teeth would splinter from their constant chattering.

"Did you enjoy your afternoon?" Peng's lantern cut through the inky darkness.

Jun glared in response as her eyes fought to adjust to the flame's assault.

"No comments? I'm shocked. You usually riddle me with questions." Setting the lantern at his feet he stood with his hands on his hips and scowled down at her. "Aren't you even curious to know what is happening back on Pandang?"

Jun got to her feet. Her shoulders rounded against the cold. "Where is Captain Quinn?"

"Hundreds of ships have crammed their way into your harbor, and he's your only concern?"

"You said you were bringing him here." Jun notched her chin and fought against the trembling in her jaw. "I want to see him."

Peng leaned forward and stared. "You bloody well care for the man." The peak of his eyebrows heightened. "I knew you rutted with the bastard, but I never imagined you could have feelings for him."

"Where is he?" Jun ground the words between clenched teeth.

"Most unfortunate news, I'm afraid. He's escaped."

A ray of relief warmed her heart. "He *bested* you." Pride in Will's innate skills made her grin.

"No," Peng snapped in defense. "He bested your men. Killed two of them in the process and disappeared into the night." Peng stroked his beard and laughed. "Evidently, he didn't share quite the same feelings for you. One whiff of freedom and he was happy to get as far away from you as he could."

"I'm glad." Jun crossed her arms over her chest. "He'll live, and you can spend the rest of your days constantly looking over your shoulder. Wondering when he'll return."

"Don't you mean *if* he'll return? Another nice fantasy, Jun. But with nine hundred ships and more than forty-thousand men at my disposal, I'm sure we'll find him before too long. Westerners don't hide well in this part of the world." Peng tipped his head. "Did I tell you about the others? You know," he tapped the side of his chin. "I'm sure I haven't. In all the excitement, it must have slipped my mind."

Jun straightened. The mental tug of war with him was making her weary mind stumble. What the hell was he up to? He was toying with her like a spider with a fly. She had to focus.

He hadn't drawn a weapon on her yet, but he was heavily armed. His always-present pistol. His side cutlass. Jun had witnessed that blade's deadly edge. And, of course, the amethyst bejeweled dirk he carried in his boot, more a fashion accessory than a weapon. If she could just keep her wits about her and get her hands on the hilt of that sword. "What others?"

"Survivors from his ship. Three more of them." Peng shook his head. "I've held them prisoner since I scuttled what was left of their ship. I had such plans, you see. I wanted to surprise Captain Quinn with our famous Dragon's Fire hospitality before bringing him here. I'm sure he would have enjoyed watching what was left of his crew lose their heads one by one."

"You really are a vile bastard."

"Of course I am, you trained me to be the best." Peng bent to pick up the lantern. "I must be honest, I'm a bit disappointed. Now knowing how deeply you feel for him, it would have made killing him in front of you so satisfying."

Peng never took his eyes from her as he stepped backward to the door. The smile on his face sent an uneasy fear down Jun's spine.

He knocked on the door and continued, "But you know, ruling an empire this size takes nothing if not the ability to adapt to every situation that arises. Not being able to enjoy the look on your lovely face as you watch me end Captain Quinn's life, it only made me adjust my plans slightly."

The door opened and Peng broke eye contact with Jun long enough to grab someone from the darkened galley way and haul them into the room.

Ting and Qi clung to one another as they fell in a huddled mess at Jun's feet.

Jun rushed to help them up. One of Ting's eyes was almost swollen shut. Qi's grip on her mother was so tight, Jun couldn't separate them. Both of them looked at her, their eyes filled with terror.

"You bastard!" Jun lunged at Peng. Her hands curled into claws. She'd tear his eyes from his skull.

Swinging the lantern, he caught her across the cheek with the heavy brass base, knocking her to one side while he pulled one of his pistols and leveled it at Ting and Qi. "Stay back or I'll shoot them both with one shot!"

* * * *

Anger drove Will to be the first man over the rails of Jun's ship, followed closely by Dowd. For the twentieth time in as many minutes, he thanked whatever fates had brought his old crewmate to him again. Will could sail the *Scarlet Night* practically one-handed, but a junk was another ship entirely. Had it not been for Dowd, Will would still be spinning in a tight circle trying to navigate his way out of Pandang harbor.

With so much traffic, they hadn't had any trouble "borrowing" a small two-masted vessel. Even with its squared hull and a direct head wind, they had flown over the waves.

They spotted Jun's ship not too long after losing sight of Pandang's shores. There was little question that the grand, gold-tipped ship was hers. As Will suspected, Peng hadn't traveled far, just far enough to move back and forth from Pandang and keep Jun out of sight of the rest of her men. They were anchored in one of the deep coves off the western coast of Salahnama. The steep cliff shores of the island rose straight up from the sea. Had anyone tried to escape the ship, they'd have nowhere to go.

On the way, Dowd had drawn the odd setup of the decks below. Junks weren't a series of decks like a western ship. They were set up more like a ship of boxes so that if one section was damaged in a fight and took on water, the rest of the ship would remain tight, but this meant navigating bulkheads and ladder ways that had little similarity to the *Scarlet Night*.

Will didn't care. All he wanted was to find Jun. Slit Peng's throat in the process, but find her…safe. They'd come in dark to swing in as close to Jun's ship as they dared. Climbing the anchor chain had been easy when fury burned in your belly.

He pulled the boarding sword he still carried and crouched in the shadows until he was joined by the others. He held up three fingers and pointed toward the ship's bow, indicating the three men at their posts there. Four more guarded aft. All were heavily armed by what Will could see.

He tapped Hills and Higgins to take out the forward men. Will, Dowd, and Griffin would tend to the four. Will signed, *'No pistols.'* Gunfire would alert any men below. They were already outnumbered, but these were good men, and Will trusted them to secure the upper deck.

They stuck all at once. Will swung his boarding sword low across one man's knees. The poor bastard didn't know what hit him. Will delivered the killing blow and swung to engage the next. Dowd had another man on the ground, his boot threatening to crush the man's windpipe. Dowd had inflicted a killing slice across the man's chest. Griffin was dancing with the other two, his back against the aft mast. He didn't have to dance alone for long. Hills and Higgins had made short work of their dance partners and came to his rescue.

The man under Dowd's boot was losing blood fast.

Will looked down into the man's graying face and gestured to Dowd. *'Ask him…where's Jian Jun?'* The dying man pressed bloodied lips together and refused to answer. Dowd increased the pressure of his foot before asking him again. The man pointed a finger and answered Dowd.

Dowd signed, *'One deck down. Aft cabin. Two guards. Chou Peng is with her.'*

Will's focus narrowed to a pinpoint. His white-hot anger had turned black. He traded his short sword for a twin-edged cutlass and headed aft. It was time to kill this bastard and be done with it.

He slid down the ladder without taking a single rung. A narrow passageway separated the walled sections of the deck. Little light reached into the dark, but Will could see a faint glow coming from the rear of the ship. There wouldn't be much room to fight in these tight quarters. The secret was going to be getting in without trapping himself.

Stomping his feet, he kicked at one of the partitions, then stood back into the depth of the shadows behind the ladder and waited. One of the guards came forward to investigate. He and Will had a short intense meeting that ended in Will dragging the man's body away from the passageway.

Will knocked against the wall again.

This time when the second guard came forward, he rushed to his crewmate's side only to meet the hilt end of Will's cutlass in a sharp blow to his temple. He crumpled over his friend's body like cheap parchment.

Will's heart fisted blood through his veins as he eased his way toward the glow, sword drawn. If the man on deck had lied...

The door in front of him was deeply carved with the winding figure of a dragon. Gold and cinnabar flames reached out from his gaping mouth.

Will reached over to the lantern burning low in its hanger and extinguished the light, tightened his hand over the leather-wrapped handle of his sword, and groped in the dark for the door's handle.

He looked over his shoulder into the black abyss behind him before leveraging the iron latch. A splinter of shifting light pierced the dark. Will's heart slowed with the practiced skill of a trained warrior. He channeled the cold detachment of a killer stalking his prey. But then he saw them.

Opening the door wider, the sight inside dropped a curtain of red over that chilled restraint. Jun was on her knees, blood ran down her cheek. Peng's back was to the door. A lantern swung from one hand, the other held a pistol aimed directly at...*fuck*...

The bastard had returned to Pandang after Will and the men had left to steal the junk and found Ting and Qi. Ting held the child, doing her best to twist and curl her body over her daughter to protect her from the madman about to shoot them.

Jun got to her feet. She held her arms wide. Bringing Peng's attention back to her. Will slowly opened the door a bit wider.

Pistol, lantern, side sword, dirk. Peng wore a baldric. He could have as many as two other pistols strapped to his chest. Will couldn't remember seeing him wear that many weapons, but he couldn't take the chance. At best, he still had one shot. At this range, Peng wouldn't miss his mark.

Will noticed something else—a mere second before Peng noticed the same thing. Cold air. The temperature in the hallway was much cooler, and the rush of chilled air into the room spun Peng around.

The man was quick to swing the pistol's business end in Will's direction before lifting the lantern to find him standing in the doorway.

Sword raised, Will was no match for a pistol, but that didn't stop him from taking a step toward Peng. His baldric didn't hold any more guns. The man only had one shot, and Will would gladly take it. The bastard better make it a clean kill, or he'd be on him before the smoke cleared.

Instead, Peng turned back and aimed the pistol at Jun's head. The air rushed out of Will's lungs. *No...you cowardly slime, shoot me!* He froze where he stood.

Peng looked back and forth between him and Jun. After the initial panicked look in his eye, Will saw the pleasured sneer as Peng said something to Jun. Will dared a fleeting glance at her, but in that second, he saw a lifetime of emotions cross her face. Relief, fear, pain, hate, anger, pleading, love.

Will's resolve tightened in his gut. Peng was a dead man. He lowered his chin, and returned his battle focus to getting these women the hell out of there. The muscle in his jaw pulsed with a steeled determination. *Patience...wait for it...*

Peng's mouth continued to move. One advantage of being deaf, Will could not be distracted by whatever vile waste was falling from the man's lips. It wouldn't spur a reckless reaction. It wouldn't alter his focus in any way. Will would lay coin on the fact that Peng wasn't praising his escape skills or bargaining for his life. Will inched closer. Crowding Peng would make him nervous and nervous men made mistakes.

He was shouting now. Eyes wild, the veins in Peng's neck bulged with the effort. He pushed the pistol harder toward Jun and glared at the tip of Will's sword. Pointing with the hand still holding the lantern toward the floor, spittle flew from Peng's mouth. The pistol was cocked.

Peng wanted his sword on the floor, or Jun was dead.

Chapter 25

The gash in Jun's cheek burned. She could taste the rusty tang of blood in her mouth. Will filled the doorway. The lantern's light still swayed, catching the glint off his bloodied blade raised to end Peng's miserable life.

But Peng had been too quick. His lust for revenge had poisoned his senses. He hadn't realized it yet, but he was surrounded. The only thing keeping him alive was one pull of the trigger. When Will's gaze met hers for that split second, she knew. He wasn't leaving until Peng was dead. She saw something else too. Something worth risking everything for.

He loved her.

Peng's shouts echoed in the empty cabin. "Drop your sword or I'll end her life now."

"Scream all you want, he can't hear you," Jun taunted.

"Shut your mouth." He waved the lantern and screeched again. "Drop your fucking sword, you stupid bastard!"

Jun watched Will lower his blade to the floor and hold his arms wide. If he could hold Peng's attention for another second…

"Kick it to me." Peng swung his foot in frustration. "It's like communicating with a damn rock."

Will pushed the sword away from him with the toe of his boot. Jun smiled. He'd offered Peng the blade end. If they both lunged for the weapon, Will still kept the advantage. "He has more brains in his little toe than you have in your entire crew."

"Shut up." Peng moved forward and wrapped his arm around her in order to keep his pistol threateningly close to her face and ease forward enough to kick the sword away from Will.

Will's eyes never left Peng. He didn't move. The cold, dark intensity in his gaze made even Jun shiver. She'd known all along he was a warrior.

To see it for herself was quite another thing.

"Where the hell are my men? He couldn't have killed them all."

"His dripping blade says otherwise."

Peng tightened his hold. "Too bad he didn't think to bring a pistol."

"Too bad you didn't think to bring two."

"Shut. Up." The barrel of his gun dug into the space behind her jawbone. "It will only take one shot to end you."

Jun warned, "And one second after for him to be on you. You don't stand a chance."

Peng lowered the lantern to the floor, bending her with him, and pulled the dirk from his boot with his free hand. "Then the bullet will be for him, and I'll just have to slit your throat instead." He straightened and adjusted the position of the gun.

"Aim true." Jun continued to taunt him. Sweat broke out on Peng's forehead. She was getting to him.

"Oh, I intend to. Right after I finish off your maid and her little idiot brat." Peng turned his head to look toward Ting and Qi. Jun watched in horror as Qi scuttled across the floor like a crab across a hot beach. The child snatched Will's sword, and slid it to him before ducking between his legs.

In one impetuous move, Peng swung his pistol and fired, but Will had dropped to grab his sword and Peng's precious lone bullet did little but shatter the wood in the door frame behind Will.

With the shot still ringing in her ears, Jun saw her chance, and reached across Peng's body to pull hard on the hilt of his side cutlass. The strength of the pull shifted his body around toward her as she yanked the weapon from its sheath. His foot caught the lantern on the floor and kicked it to shatter against the wall.

Smoke and sulphur from the pistol burned her nose. Peng threw the gun aside and made a wide sweep at her with his dirk, but it was too late. She had him.

With both hands tight to the grip, Jun lunged at him, catching Peng in his lower gut. She buried the blade as deep as she could then used her body's momentum to draw the sword higher as she came up under his arm.

Standing nose to nose with him, Peng looked at her in shock. His mouth opening and closing like a fish, before the dirk clattered to the floor behind her.

"You missed, you stupid fool. Now you're dead." She gave one final twist to the blade and sneered into his ugly face. "Are you watching me now?"

Peng's body crumbled against hers as Will reached her. He shoved the weight of Peng off her. Blood soaked her front and down her thighs. Will didn't stop to find out if any of it was hers.

The lantern had started a fire. Its flames were already racing up the side of the dry bamboo walls. Hot, black smoke blanketed the ceiling.

Will pushed Ting and Qi out of the room before he scooped Jun into his arms and followed close at their heels. They met four men coming from the other direction.

Jun could hear the fire's anger behind them as it feasted on the back cabin.

One of the men grabbed Qi and nearly threw her up the ladder way. He pushed Ting up behind her then stood aside to let Will try to navigate with her still in his arms. Jun pushed out of his arms and ascended without aid. Will's hand never left her back. She joined Ting and Qi in the bow. Bodies littered the deck around her.

Will and the other men hurried to lay a boarding ladder across the span of water to a smaller junk waiting alongside. The first flames licked up from the tail of the ship. If they didn't get away, the fire would soon claim the other ship.

As with the ladder way, one of the men saw to Qi and Ting. He pushed Ting ahead and lifted Qi into his arms before carrying her across.

Two of the other men didn't wait for the ladder. They swung instead on ropes to drop onto the deck of the smaller junk and began to untie the clew lines holding the corners of the sails.

Jun was next across, then came the last of Will's men. Flames totally engulfed the back end of her once beautiful junk. Will stood silhouetted against the fire's glow, then he was all at once in her arms.

No sooner had his feet touched the deck, but the men boomed the sails to catch the wind and the little junk leapt forward through the water.

Will cradled her face in his hands, gently fingering the small gash marring her cheek, before running his touch over her body. Did he think some of the blood staining her clothing was? She caught his wrists and shook her head. "I'm fine. I'm fi—"

His mouth claimed hers as he wrapped her tight in an embrace and kissed her soundly. With her arms around his neck, Jun clung to him, tugging on his beautiful hair. His lips bruising hers with the force of his kisses. Will lifted her off her feet and crushed her to him. He held her as if he'd never let her go. Her heart soared with the thought that he never had to.

"Ahem…" A man standing nearby cleared his throat.

Will heard no interruption and continued to deepen his kiss. Jun pulled back and laid her fingertips over his lips before pointing shyly at the man.

The glare Will shot in his direction made Jun laugh.

"Beggin' Capt'n's pardon," the man made a few gestures as he spoke.

"Where the hell we be goin? Back to Pandang?"

Will nodded, *'Yes.'*

Jun answered, "No."

"Bloody hell." The man planted his hands on his hips. "Not bad enough that I been shipwrecked, imprisoned, beaten, battled, and nearly roasted." He flung a hand toward the burning ship behind them. "Now I get to take orders from two bloody Captains." He crossed his arms over the broad span of his chest and leveled them both a glare of his own. "Make up yer minds. I just need to be knowin' which way te point this square-nosed tub."

"South, Mister...?"

"Griffin, ma'am." He tugged at the front of his hair as if tipping a cap.

"South, please, Mister Griffin. And ten degrees east if you don't mind."

He tugged at his forelock again. "I don't mind a bit, ma'am." He gave Will a playful shove on his shoulder. "Carry on."

Ting and Qi were having their own reunion. The man holding Qi had pulled Ting into his arms as well.

Griffin huffed at them. "At ease, Dowd, get yer arse to them sails and work that junk magic only you seem to know."

The man kissed Qi's forehead and handed the child back to her mother. Even had Jun not heard his name, she would have recognized the resemblance between him and his daughter.

"Dowd?" Jun raised her eyebrows at Ting, who flushed to the roots of her hair.

"Aye, mistress," Ting watched her man head toward the forward mast. "My Dowd."

Leaving Will's embrace, Jun crossed to Ting. The women hugged tightly, before Jun knelt and hugged Qi. "One day soon I will learn how to make all the signs I need to tell you how grateful I am that you are so smart and brave. Until then I do know how to say, 'Thank you.'" Jun repeated the sign three times before pulling Qi in for another tight hug.

When she looked up, Will was nodding his own approval at the girl. Qi beamed at him.

Then he held out his hand to Jun and led her away from the others. Together they climbed the short stairs to the raised deck along the back of the junk.

Again he fingered the wound at her cheek until she lifted his hand and kissed his palm.

"I'm fine."

Will made some gestures, and looked about them shaking his head. He held his hand flat and mimicked writing.

Jun shrugged her shoulders. The treasured writing slate was miles away by now. "I'm sure there is something on this ship we can use." When she attempted to start her quest, he stopped her. His eyes held hers as his hands flew in a rapid succession of gestures. She missed almost all, but the message was repeated in the series of expressions that crossed his face.

Will paused. He reached out to trace the line of her lip, frowning. She wished she could understand. His frustration mirrored her own. Then he held her hand and gently tugged at her arm. He pushed back her sleeve and tapped a finger on the tender skin of her wrist.

Slowly, he ran the tip of that finger across her skin. Pointing to himself, he repeated the motion. *'I'* He looked at her expectantly before continuing. *'L'*

Will was using her arm as a writing stone.

'O,' 'V,'

Jun's eyes flew to his. He shook his head and tapped her arm again, bringing her attention back to his writing.

He ran the side of his hand over her skin as if erasing the letters. He began again.

I, L, O, V, E, Y, O, U

When she lifted her eyes again, there it was written as clearly in his eyes as it was upon her skin. He loved her.

"I love you, too. So much, so very, very much."

Will lowered his gaze to her mouth. Jun shook her head and reached for his arm instead.

I, L, O, V, E, Y, O, U Jun released her hold on him just long enough to sign *'more'*.

Chapter 26

As the pale pink beginnings of the dawn stretched across the sky, Will and Jun stood in the bow of the ship.

Griffin soon joined them. Jun was grateful to have him and Dowd along to help translate. Although, she and Will had little trouble communicating all through the night. Her skin still tingled. He'd written *'I love you'* over the crest of her breast. *'I love you'* along the inside of her thigh. Across the small of her back. Down the flat of her belly. He'd marked her. Like the tattoo she wore, she now wore his words as well and would feel them on her skin and within her soul all the days of her life.

"How are we supposed to find an island that isn't even on a map?" Griffin grumbled.

"Because I've been there before and will guide you."

Will's hands flew. Griffin explained. "He wants to know why you're doing this?"

She started to tell Griffin, but he was just the interpreter. Looking back at Will, she answered his question. "Because it's time." Jun slipped her hand into Will's. "I've spent my life fighting and scraping to stay at the top. Years of hard work. It was all I had. It was my identity."

"Not so fast…" Griffin's hands struggled over a few of the signs.

"Sorry." She squeezed Will's hand. "The fire on Fu's junk was my chance. Jian Jun is dead. She perished along with her trusted first mate, Chou Peng." Jun made the sign for a term she'd learned last night from Dowd to describe Peng. *'Rat Bastard.'*

Will's gaze broke from hers to watch Griffin's signs. He looked back at her and signed. Griffin spoke over her shoulder. "He says, What about your fleet? Your empire?"

She waited to gaze into his eyes again. "I don't have to go back for the fleet to go on. Pandang harbor was full of hundreds of ships. I'm sure by now the dragon has eight new heads. It's time to walk away. If I go back, I may never get another chance." She put her hand over Will's heart. "It's time to live my life. Mine. Not my dead husband's. It was out of respect for him I stepped into his boots, but I lost who I was along the way."

She paused again before stroking Will's chest. "You showed me who I am. Who I've wanted to be all my life."

"And you want us to walk away with you?" The question came from Dowd.

Jun turned to answer him. Her gaze looked at each man. "You are all free to do what you want. Stay. Go. You have served me with loyalty all these years, Mister Dowd, and I have stolen that time away from your family. I give it back to you." She looked at Griffin, Hills, and Higgins. "And you have been wronged by my people. I owe you a debt as well. You came to my rescue out of respect for your captain." She gazed back into Will's handsome eyes. "Such devotion should be rewarded." She smiled at Ting and Qi. "And you are my family. I want nothing but your happiness." Jun waved her hand to indicate them all. "I can see to it you all live the rest of your lives in comfort. I am a very wealthy woman."

"Were a wealthy woman. Ain't ye dead now?" Hills noted.

A smile tipped her mouth. "That is why we are headed to a tiny island nestled between Bangka and Belitung. It has no name, no inhabitants, but Fu called it our nest within a nest."

"Nest within a nest?" Dowd asked.

Will frowned at her as well as the rest.

"Yes, it's very difficult to find, and even harder to navigate a ship into her lagoon. It's almost completely surrounded by a wide coral reef."

Higgins shook his head and turned away. "I've had me fill o'reefs. Can't be nothin' worth riskin' another try at drownin'."

"Even for eight chests filled with more gold than we could all spend in eight lifetimes?"

Higgins turned around. "I be listenin'."

"Fu called it our nest egg. Insurance. If we lost the fleet. Lost our power. We would always have this treasure. He buried it after we were wed. We're the only two people who know where it lies." She looked up at Will. "That is until I met you. You know its exact location."

* * * *

Hours later, Will issued the order to drop anchor after their small crew threaded the needle into Jun's nest within a nest. At her insistence, he was the only one to accompany her through the pale aquamarine water to the white sands of a small lagoon on the north side of her mystery island. She'd made the rest promise to give her and Will some private time before they joined them to start digging.

Crawling out of the surf, they laid on the warmth of the sand.

Tell me the secret now?

Soon. Jun traced the words in the wet sand next to his.

No hint?

Jun looked at him and smiled that tender little smile that caught his heart and sent a jolt of heat straight to his loins. She straddled him and kissed him before climbing off and offering a beautiful view of her back as she slowly removed her wet sandy clothing. Jun walked naked into the warm water. When she emerged a few moments later, she looked like some mythical goddess rising from the sea itself. Her skin glowed in the late afternoon light.

She came and stood by him where he sat on the shore, letting him drink in the sight of her beautiful body. With the tip of her toe, she scrawled the single word *Secret* into the sand.

With her naked before him, it was difficult to think beyond his desire to make love to her. What secret? What was she trying to say?

Taking his hand, she ran it down over the curve of her hip, bringing it to rest on the pale petals of her lotus tattoo.

The lotus? He knew all about her tattoo. She'd explained it to him on their first night together. He shook his head, still confused.

And then Jun began tracing the delicate lines with her fingers in slow erotic strokes before stopping and pointing to the center swirl of the design. Lifting his hand, she put his finger where hers stopped. Heat rushed to his erection. He wrapped his arm around her thighs and kissed the patterned flesh beneath his touch.

She trembled before lowering herself to the sand beside him, then kissed him and turned to write in the sand with the sharp edge of a shell. *This island is laid out like this lotus. I carry the map. That is why none have seen it but the man who hid the treasure, and now the man who claims it.*

Will looked deep into her eyes. He loved her, but what she was proposing was beyond his wildest imaginings. *Are you sure about all this?*

She frowned and shook her head. *Sure about what? Loving you? I've no choice in that.*

He leaned in to kiss her and licked the salt water from her lips. Will pulled back and wrote. *Sharing your wealth with me. Giving up your fleet. Your empire. Not too late to turn back.*

Jun shook her head and added below his words. *Never going back.*

Don't give it up for me.

Not giving up anything. She cupped his cheek. *You're my life, my heart. My everything.*

And you're mine.

Will pulled her to him and rolled so she was lying along his body. Never in all his years did he ever imagine being completely and hopelessly in love with a woman. This woman. Powerful, beautiful, fierce woman. Swinging a cutlass and ruling tens of thousands of men and women one day, and making love to him tenderly the next, it stole his breath.

Yes, he had known love before, but it was a young man's crush compared to what he felt for Jun. He had been willing to die for Samantha. With Jun he wanted to live to be a very old man so he could spend a lifetime with her.

Will stroked the side of his chin with his thumb before clasping his hands together. *'Be my wife.'* Jun watched him carefully. She'd gotten in the habit of trying to guess what his signs meant.

She patted the sand and wrote,

You're hungry for clams?

The corner of his mouth tipped. *Guess again.*

You want me to hold your hand?

Something like that.

She lifted one shoulder. *I give up.*

Will worked Tupper's ring off his hand. He'd promised to never take it off again after it had brought him luck at the gaming tables. But if he ever believed in the promise of finding the love of your life, he had Tupper Quinn to thank. The love she shared with Gavin stayed with her until the very end. Will suspected she'd approve of him giving Jun her ring.

He slipped Tupper's ring onto Jun's finger. *Marry me.*

Her breath left her in a rush. Will could feel her heart racing over his. He lifted his fist and bent his wrist. *That's how you sign 'yes.'*

'Yes, yes, yes, yes, yes.'

Jun pulled Will to his feet and led him into the grove of trees just off the beach and showed him how each stood in the same position as the points of the petals on the lotus she wore.

Together they'd claimed a treasure worth more than a thousand chests of gold. They had found and fought and loved one another. And now they were both free to sail into a future open with possibilities, clear skies by day, and all the passion in each other's arms by night.

Who could guess where they might end their days? As long as they could boast fair winds, following seas, routes that ran true, and plenty of rum…the adventure might never end.

Author's Note

It is with a very bittersweet heart that I write the last chapter of the Captains of the Scarlet Night Series. All along the way, I have thanked people for their help, support, and encouragement. Now I want to thank my readers, for without you this book might never have been written.

When I wrote Within A Captain's Hold, I had no way of knowing the extent of the adventure I'd embarked upon. Through each chapter, each story, I fell more and more in love with these amazing characters who graciously allowed me to slip my feet into their boots and sail away with them. I wanted them to come alive for you, as they had for me.

Even at that, I never intended to write William Quinn's story, but "Bump" grew in my heart and in the hearts of my readers. I will forever be grateful for the gentle…okay not so gentle, push to write his final adventure. I can honestly say, this has been the most challenging book I've ever written.

Will's character has given me the unique opportunity to step inside a community I may never have been exposed to. I wish to give sincere and undying gratitude to the members of the deaf community who have helped me to understand Will's life a little better.

I pray that I have honored your trust in me to bring you this amazing character. I hope he is a true and worthy representative of the amazing people I have met and continue to meet who tell me Will "Bump" Quinn has touched a place in their hearts.

I know, he will forever hold a place in mine.

Thank you all so very much. I love you all!

Lisa……

Within A Captain's Power

Read on for a special sneak peek of the previous book in the Captains of the Scarlet Night series!

Never underestimate the power of a pirate . . .

Captain James Steele is duty bound to capture the privateer Scarlet Night and bring her rebellious crew to England to hang. Then he will leave his majesty's service, make an upstanding marriage, and join the landed gentry. But the winds of fate are blowing the straitlaced commander utterly off course.

Once aboard, James comes face to face with a pirate boy who is in reality fierce, desperate—and gorgeous—Samantha Christian, on the run from a sadistic Virginia plantation owner. With her identity unbound, the good captain dutifully takes her under his personal command, whereupon decorum goes out the porthole. But while his heart is lost to Samantha by the time they reach England, her noose still awaits. Now James's sense of duty will be severely tested. As for Samantha, she has a plan, and a duty, of her own . . .

Learn more about Lisa A. Olech
http://www.kensingtonbooks.com/author.aspx/31711

Chapter 1

Pleasant Ridge, Virginia — 1715

"Are you trying to get yourself killed?"

"I'm buying myself some time." Samantha Christian whispered behind her fan.

"You're buying yourself another beating." Her companion, Rebecca Whitmore, whispered back.

"As long as I know it will be the last, Wessler can do his worst."

The air in the Whitmore's ballroom was stifling. The room was packed with an overabundance of Virginia's beautifully dressed elite. Plantation owners with their gossiping wives and pampered daughters wearing their latest Parisian fashions. Political bigwigs vying for attention, and high-ranking British military in crisp, sharp uniforms. All these, and Samantha—in the ill-fitting, cast-off gown of Damian Wessler's deceased wife. She did her best to blend into the silk damask wallpaper. A mighty challenge wearing the color puce.

It was the annual harvest ball. An anticipated favorite in the surrounding community. It would be social suicide not to attend, which is why Wessler agreed to allow Samantha to come, even though he despised her burgeoning friendship with Isabelle Whitmore and her daughter Rebecca.

"Fine. We'll go. But I won't be spending my money on some foolish new gown. One of Marlene's will do." He snatched at her upper arm and gripped it viciously. Samantha shook with the effort not to cry out. "And if I catch you talking to those blasted Whitmore bitches, or you embarrass me in the slightest way, you'll live to regret it." He spit between his clenched teeth.

It was his favorite expression. *"You'll live to regret it."* There was much Samantha regretted, but it did her little good to go back and try to undo what had already been done. Her only other option was to put her plan in action to leave the vile prison she found herself in, regardless of the unavoidable risk to her health. Wessler's beating tonight would happen whether she followed his strict dictate or not. She might as well earn it honestly.

Samantha fanned at her cheeks. She and Rebecca stood tucked in amongst the huge floral arrangements decorating the room. Magnolias and dogwood perfumed the space. She caught Wessler glaring at them from across the room and massaged the nauseous pitch and roll of her stomach with gloved fingers.

"Mother has sent word, but if the *Scarlet Night* has moved on from their hiding place..." Rebecca clutched at Samantha's wrist. Pale eyes, wide with concern, met hers.

Samantha smiled, trying to reassure the girl. "That's a chance I'll have to take." She closed her fan with a snap, kissed Rebecca's cheek, and shot a defiant smile in Damian Wessler's direction. "Now, why don't you introduce me to the handsome Captain Steele?"

Captain James Steele of the Royal British Navy was among the guests at tonight's ball. He cut a dashing figure in his dress uniform of navy and cream. Broad shoulders filled his gold-trimmed coat. Brass buttons winked in the flicker of the hundreds of candles lighting the room. He wore no wig, choosing to club his hair. The color was a rich auburn that shone to a light ginger in the candlelight. It made the blue of his eyes all the more striking. Taller than the majority, he was by far the most noticeable man in the room.

After the proper introductions, he swept her onto the dance floor. "Have you lived in Virginia long, Mistress Christian?"

Her gaze darted from Wessler's livid glare to the handsomeness of Captain Steele. "Six months. However, it feels more like six years."

He grinned. The curve of his mouth revealed a slight dimple in his left cheek. "Do you miss your home so much?"

"I do, and my family most of all." She tried to concentrate on the steps of the dance and boost her fortitude.

"I, as well, but soon I'll happily set sail with orders bringing me back to England. I'm looking forward to autumn in Weatherington."

"Weatherington? Is that where you're from?" She dared another glance in Wessler's direction. His glower caused her to falter and step on the captain's polished boot. "I-I grew up not too far from there in South Oxbridge."

Captain Steele never missed a beat. "You don't say. I know South Oxbridge well." He spun her to the music before dipping his head and dropping his voice almost to a whisper. "I must warn you, my lady, there is a gentleman standing off my port side who has the most disagreeable scowl directed at us."

Samantha could almost feel Wessler's eyes burning holes through her back. She forced a grin. "Does he resemble an overfed hound dog in a wig?"

The captain threw back his head and laughed. The sound warmed her clear through and somehow gave her a necessary measure of courage. "Why, yes, now that you mention it, there is something a bit hound dog about him. Who is he? A suitor perhaps? An overprotective uncle? By his expression, perhaps he is your betrothed?"

She lifted her gaze from his pristine silk neckcloth. The Captain's eyes were impossibly blue. They were the sky on a brilliant summer afternoon. "No, he is not my betrothed. He is more my jailer."

Captain Steele laughed again. "Isn't that somewhat the same thing?"

"Spoken like a man who is either terminally single or unhappily betrothed."

"Betrothed, but not unhappily. Impatient. I'm to be wed as soon as I return to England."

Samantha blinked at the quick rush of unexpected disappointment. "Congratulations, Captain. Your fiancée is a lucky woman indeed."

"Thank you. Lillian is lovely. We're well matched."

"Will you wed in Weatherington?"

"Unfortunately, no. Lillian lives in London. She does not share my love of the country. A bit too rustic for her tastes."

"I'm a true country girl, I'm afraid," Samantha lifted a shoulder in a slight shrug, "but I've always longed to see London."

His rust-tinged brows rose. "You didn't sail from there?"

"No, Portsmouth." Turning once more in the dance, Samantha caught Wessler heading toward them, only to be intercepted by one of the other local plantation owners. He acknowledged the man with a civilized nod. The tolerant set of his jaw told Samantha he'd been caught in conversation. He shot her another dark scowl.

"Well, if you ever find yourself back in England, you must allow me to show you London."

Captain Steele's warm voice softened the edge of Wessler's threat. "Won't your Lillian mind?" She blinked up at him.

The dimple in his cheek flashed once more. "I suspect she'd frown like your guard dog."

"I can certainly understand why. You are quite handsome." A darting look told her Wessler still watched. Samantha laid her hand on the lapel of the captain's jacket. "What is it about a man in uniform that is so appealing?" She traced the gold braid.

"I wouldn't know. I'm surrounded by men in uniform every day. I fail to see the allure."

Samantha's laugh sounded tinny and forced to her ear. Their dance ended. Couples began to clear the dance floor. Wessler finished his conversation and seemed intent on making his way through the crowd toward them once again.

"Captain, I do beg your pardon, but I am suddenly feeling a bit...It's so terribly warm..." She feigned a stumble.

He caught her arm. "Are you unwell?"

"Air." She lifted a shaky hand to her throat. "I'm desperate for a bit of air."

The orchestra began another lively tune. New dancers crowded the floor and blocked Wessler's approach as Captain Steele guided her quickly in the opposite direction toward the French doors leading to the back veranda.

The night breeze was a blessed relief after the heat of the ballroom. Moving them into the shadows, Samantha pressed a hand to her ribs and drew in several deep breaths. She lifted the back of her hand to her cheek.

Captain Steele gave her a worried frown. "Are you all right?"

"Yes," she nodded, "I believe so." She shot a glance over her shoulder.

"Can I fetch you some water, perhaps?"

"No, thank you. I'm feeling much better." She laid a hand on his sleeve. The lights from the ballroom filtered through the sheer fabric adorning the doors and accented the attractive angles of his face. "Are you always so kind, Captain?"

He gave her another small grin. "Unless I'm ordered otherwise."

"You *are* in His Majesty's service." Samantha responded coyly and curtseyed.

"Aye, and loyal to king and country." He inclined his head in a small bow.

"And steadfast in your duty?" she teased.

Captain Steele stood tall. "I know of no other way."

The doors to the veranda flew open. Music and the hum of conversation tumbled out as Damian Wessler rushed from the ballroom. He stood for a moment at the railing, peering into the shadowed pathways of the Whitmore's formal gardens.

Blood rushed in Samantha's ears. Fear and panic caused her to clutch at Captain Steele's sleeves. "Forgive me, sir." she whispered before rising on tiptoes to crush her mouth to his.

"Madam—" Captain Steele put his hands to her waist and gently tried to push her away.

Samantha heard Wessler's curse behind her. She tightened her grip. "Please, Captain, I've no time to explain," She rushed. "Play along." She slipped her arm about his neck, angled her mouth, and kissed him again.

Wessler's boot heels punctuated each stride as he marched toward them.

He wrenched her out of Captain Steele's grasp. "What in the bloody hell—" he snapped. His eyes held a murderous rage as he growled into Samantha's face. His jowls trembled with barely contained fury.

Samantha wiped at the corner of her mouth. She flashed Wessler a coy smile. "You can't blame me for stealing a simple kiss." She shot a nervous glance at the Captain. In the dim light, she couldn't read his face, but the increasing bite of Wessler's fingers interrupted all else.

She faked a small stumble and a tiny burp. A forced giggle through her gloved fingertips capped her performance. "Whatever was in the punch? I'm so lightheaded."

"You'll pardon us, sir, but Mistress Christian," he jerked her to his side, "and I need to bid you a good eve." As he spoke, his grip continued to tighten. "Come along, my *dear*," he snarled as he jerked at her arm. "Didn't I warn you not to drink too much this evening? Time to get you home."

Samantha pushed at his punishing hand. "We shouldn't be rude to the Whitmore's distinguished guest." She shot Captain Steele an embarrassed glance. He was watching the exchange between her and Wessler. A frown knit his brows. "Another dance, Captain?"

"We're leaving," bit Wessler.

"The spirits were rather potent tonight. Perhaps, Mistress Christian simply needs a bit more air, Mister...?" Captain Steele held out his hand.

Damian had to release her arm to return the Captain's handshake. She couldn't stop the small gasp that escaped her. Her fingers wrapped around her battered skin.

"Wessler. Damian Wessler. I own the Blackwater Plantation. Mistress Christian is in my employ, and she can be rather wild. Undisciplined. Ignorant to social protocol. Almost defiant." The last words he directed toward her as he reached for her once more. "If you'll excuse us."

Samantha started to thank the captain for his kindness, but Wessler jerked her away. His vise-like fingers left little room for argument. He dragged her back through the crowded ballroom and past a horrified Rebecca.

"We—we need to t-thank our hosts." She resisted the strength of his pull, casting a pleading glance back at Rebecca. She'd rushed to Isabelle's side, and now both women watched their hasty departure, concern etched on their faces.

"And give you yet another opportunity to humiliate me?" He wrenched her arm, causing her to gasp as he snarled into her ear. "Shut your fucking mouth and keep moving, or—"

"Or what? I'll live to regret it?"

Meet the Author

Lisa A. Olech is an artist/writer living in her dream house nestled among the lakes in New England. She loves getting lost in a steamy book, finding the perfect pair of sexy shoes, and hearing the laughter of her men. Being an estrogen island in a sea of testosterone makes her queen. She believes in ghosts, silver linings, the power of a man in a tuxedo, and happy endings. For more please visit lisaolech.com.

Printed in the United States
by Baker & Taylor Publisher Services